Moonlight
and Monk's Bane

Also by this Author

Relentless Society Mysteries

A Murderous Charade—Book 1
In Pursuit of the Nightingale (A companion book to the series)

Other Mystery Romance

A Revolution of Hearts
Finding Anne de Bourgh
Unforgettable
One Fell Down
Betrayed
Trapped
Missing

ENJOY A FREE EBOOK.

A French aristocrat and her betrothed, an English gentleman, are partners in the league of the Scarlet Pimpernel. Will a vengeful kidnapper destroy their happily ever after?

Follow Ronda's newsletter and get behind-the-scenes info, great deals, and this **EXCLUSIVE** suspenseful romance. Simply scan the QR code below.

Dalton and Dalton Mysteries
Book 1

Moonlight
and Monk's Bane

Ronda Gibb Hinrichsen

RKH Press L.L.C.

For Katrina

Chapter 1

1886

A LEX TOOK ONE MORE step up the gravelly surface of the extinct volcano, stopped in front of the mound of fallen trees, and took a deep breath. She held the fresh pine scent inside her for as long as her lungs could keep from releasing it then breathed in again. Despite the barren emptiness that shrouded this spot of earth in the middle of Idaho's Teton Valley, the sap and oils of the green foliage that had once lived there still lingered. Like it lived of its own accord despite the hot July sun. That fit the circumstances, Alex supposed, since the truly extraordinary—the luminal—elements she needed dwelt beneath its surface. Underground. Almost as if Mother Earth had buried, er, hidden them. And yet, why would the earth do such a thing? It wasn't like luminal life was dead.

Dead. Alex shuddered. She shook her head against the images that flashed through her mind, but the word crumbled inside her like an earthquake shattering a mountain. She must not let her emotions get away from her.

She set her jaw, rubbed the sweat from her right eyebrow with the back of her hand, and hoisted her metal specimen collection pack farther up on her back. Mary, her only daughter, might be dead, but that didn't mean Alex's determination would die with her. No matter what it cost her in time or strength or—or heart, she would find those lavatricite mushrooms and uncover the handprints of the villain who'd kidnapped and killed her Mary. Then, Alex would make him pay for what he'd done.

Ivy, Alex's black, yellow, and orange mottled cat, wrapped herself around Alex's booted right ankle.

"You can walk a few more yards."

Alex didn't expect Ivy to actually understand her; she'd observed Ivy long enough to know the cat's luminal capabilities did not extend to recognizing human language. And even if Ivy could understand her, she'd pretend she hadn't. She'd likely turn away from her the way she did when Rick, Alex's estranged husband, had been around. Rick had given Ivy to Alex for her twenty-first birthday back in 1881. He'd had a pet cat just like her when he was a boy and still missed it. So when he found Ivy alone and undernourished while he was hunting for the fabled Thunderroot, he'd hoped Ivy might fill the void in his heart and become a companion for Alex. Instead, Ivy ignored Rick and clung to Alex.

And comforted me. The unexpected thought trembled through Alex's heart the way Rick's voice had the last time she'd seen him, and she pressed her lips into a tight frown. No matter how many times people criticized her for coddling that cat, she would not let it out of her sight. Ivy would not disappear as Mary had.

Footsteps plodded through the grass behind her. Alex turned and smiled. Vera, her boarder and a fellow mystiobiologist, crested the hill. Why Vera insisted on wearing her blue and white bloomer suit and a wide-brimmed hat rather than buckskin trousers and a bush jacket as Alex did, Alex didn't know.

"Just because a woman has an adventurous heart doesn't mean she isn't a lady," Vera said whenever Alex questioned her on it, to which Alex would say," I agree. But wouldn't you rather dress more practically? Like me?"

"Maybe I will one day," she'd reply.

Vera, breathing harder than Alex was but not as hard as most fifty-year-old women would be, stopped beside Alex. "I hope I haven't held you up."

"Not at all." Alex motioned to a circle of large boulders beyond the hodgepodge of logs. Rick would have said they reminded him of Stonehenge, which he claimed had a fantastical history. Alex would have shrugged off his assumption as another one of his treasure-hunting fantasies. *Why couldn't Rick ever keep his mind on the job at hand? If he had, Mary would still be alive.*

"This volcano truly is a natural wonder," Alex said.

"I completely agree with you." Vera held out the book-sized crate she'd carried with her. It had slits in the top lid. "Alistair made such a ruckus when we stepped out from under the cover of the last grove of trees that I took a few moments to check on him."

"I thought tarantulas liked the heat when molting," Alex said.

"Alistair isn't like most tarantulas."

Alex almost smiled. Every mystiobiologist claimed some form of sensitivity toward luminal organisms, and Vera was no exception. According to her, she could look into the eyes of a diminutive creature and both understand its needs and recognize its inherent powers. When Vera first discovered Alistair perched on a rock in the canyon near Alex's Southeastern Idaho home, she believed he had healing powers. Yet without concrete evidence, the other mystiobiologists dismissed her claims. Determined to prove her theory, Vera watched Alistair constantly and carried him everywhere, hoping he might demonstrate his unique ability.

Vera and Alex climbed over the fallen logs, their boots crunching on loose pine needles, and maneuvered through the boulders that jutted from the steep mountainside. They plodded down the rocky incline, loose shale skittering beneath their feet, toward the narrow, dark tunnel. It was nestled at the center of a shallow, circular depression worn into the ancient stone. Years ago, in 1861, if Alex remembered what she'd read correctly, an explorer named David Webber had announced the opening was the entrance to what he'd termed the Cold Voice Caverns. He'd written in one of his many journals that he'd given the caverns that name because they were haunted.

Which was ridiculous. All anyone had to do was climb inside the caverns and they'd know the real reason. The inside temperature felt like winter, despite the fact that the hill above it had once spewed lava. And wind blowing through the few narrow openings into the system whirled the air like a voice. So the real question should have been, what else would he name it other than Cold Voice Caverns?

Vera set her crate in the shade of a boulder. "Hand me one end of your rope. I'll find somewhere to tie it."

Alex removed the coiled rope from her belt buckle. "Use the same log we did last time. It held quite well."

"Good thinking." While Vera secured her end of the rope, Alex knelt next to the two-foot wide opening and dropped the other end inside. *Please let me find those mushrooms today.*

"Ready?" Vera called.

Alex loosened the top of her jacket from beneath her belt, forming a pouch, and cradled Ivy inside it. "Now I am. Make sure it holds."

Vera jerked on the rope. "It's good."

Alex gave a slight nod and lowered her legs into the opening. She wrapped them around the thick rope, and slid gloved hand over gloved hand down the shaft until she reached the first marker knot. One foot. Continuing on, she reached the second knot—two feet—and the third. Judging by the last time she'd been down there, Alex knew she only had about twenty more feet to go until she reached the cavern floor, but already sweat pooled across her forehead and beneath her leather cap.

Ivy squirmed.

Five feet . . .

"Meow!" Ivy stood against Alex's chest and dug her claws into her collar bone.

"Ow!" Alex lost her grip. She slid down the rope. Frantically, she latched onto another knot. "Glow, would you?" she growled at Ivy. "This place wouldn't be so dark if you'd just light up."

Alex couldn't see Ivy's face, but she imagined Ivy staring at her as only a cat could and blinking as if she knew what Alex was talking about. Alex exhaled. If only Ivy could understand her. Maybe then she would tell her why her fur sometimes glowed.

Alex wrapped her arms and legs tighter around the rope and climbed down a few more feet. She was almost there. Fortunately, when she'd last entered the cavern, she'd set Vera's live animal trap well away from the bottom of the shaft so she wouldn't accidentally step on it when she reached the ground.

Something below her thumped.

What was that? Furrowing her brow, Alex searched down into the blackness. She listened closer. The sound had come from the direction of the trap, but it wasn't a snap, as though the trap had caught something. It wasn't a brushing, either, as if an animal had bumped into it. But then, maybe the noise wasn't connected to the trap at all. Maybe the sound had come from some other part of the cave and had echoed off the cold rock walls before it had reached her. In any case, Alex must tread carefully until she could see where she was walking.

At last, Alex's feet brushed the hard-packed earth. She pulled her miner's candlestick from her belt and shoved its spiked end into the earthen wall. Next she pulled her candle from her jacket pocket, lit it with a lucifer, and slid it into the candlestick. Flickering light spread a few feet in every direction.

Alex stepped toward where she had set the trap. It was in front of the tunnel she'd most recently explored. Though sharp rocks and stalactites hung from the ceiling just as she remembered them, the jagged earth felt grittier beneath her knee-high, low-healed gaiter boots. Had the ground changed since her last exploration? With so little sunlight in the cavern, Alex could barely see her surroundings by candlelight. Plus, the persistent scuttling noises in the tunnel distracted her from noticing any changes. The noises were probably just rodents or bats. Still, her instincts warned her to leave, even as her deeper senses heightened. The sounds had belonged to something *else*, and she really wanted to find out what that *else* was.

Alex set Ivy on the ground next to her feet. "Stay there."

Ivy didn't obey. Instead, she wrapped herself around Alex's ankle.

Alex sighed. "I guess she's coming with me."

Frowning, Alex shifted the cross-body strap holding her specimen case to a more comfortable position and again scrutinized the cavern. As before, shadows outlined the crevices along the rock walls, but there was no new plant growth.

She groaned. Where were those mushrooms? In the *Western Mystiobiologists Journal*'s 1884 spring edition, Dr. Evanston had named the fungi *Amonita lavatricite*. When scientists dried, ground, and mixed the mushrooms with salt, they discovered a method to reveal hidden luminal traces within natural elements. These traces could expose otherwise invisible substances, like handprints, hidden blood splatters, and—as Alex hoped—critical clues on objects like clothing. Dr. Evanston theorized that the fungi's mysterious power originated from magma flowing near Yellowstone, though he hadn't yet proven this connection.

Alex tilted her head. Was that the reason the mushrooms grew underground? *Hmm*. Perhaps that would be a good topic for her to discuss in her next article for the *Journal*. It might not be as important a subject as the one she would write on the lavatracites' physical and luminal properties, but such work would strengthen her credentials as a mystiobiologist and add to her limited funds.

Alex sneezed, stepped toward the second tunnel, and sneezed again. When a third sneeze didn't come, she tapped her forefinger against her chin. The air was stale and musty, but did it also contain pollen? Pollen always made her—*sneeze*!

She sniffed, brushed the back of her finger across the lower ridge of her nose, and leaned a bit farther into the darkness. If, indeed, there was pollen in this cavern, there must also be plant life. And plant life meant there must be a water source. Perhaps the mushrooms were near that water. *Or did the mushrooms create the pollen?*

Like a prayer for good luck, Alex touched the pink hair ribbon she'd tied and knotted around her left wrist—Mary's favorite. She pulled her thin scarf up from under her cotton blouse to cover her nose and mouth.

Ivy stood on her hind legs against Alex's shin. "Meow."

"Yes, we're going in there." Alex now stood about ten feet away from the tunnel's opening. It wasn't much more than four feet tall at the entrance. She hadn't looked far inside, but the passage between the stalactites and stalagmites was so narrow she might have to crawl through them. There was no way she could carry a cat. Would Ivy follow her?

Ivy sat on Alex's feet.

"You do realize the dark would disappear if you'd light up," Alex told her yet again. "You have that ability. Use it."

Ivy's green eyes reflected the candle's light, but just like before, her fur remained dark.

Alex pursed her lips. *Mental note: Ivy's fear of the dark is not connected to her luminal power—or to my insistence that she use it.* "Suit yourself," she said aloud to Ivy.

A screeching, metallic sound slid across the gritty ground.

Alex whirled to where she'd set the trap. In his article, Dr. Evanston had described encountering bizarre, unidentifiable excretions deep within these caverns, though the mysterious creature responsible had always eluded his careful tracking. Could that same elusive animal be the source of the sounds she'd just heard?

"Looks like I should have checked the trap when we first got down here, Ivy."

Alex, with Ivy staying close to her heels, inched toward the sound. No luminal tingles pulsed through her sinuses, which meant the thing wasn't a plant. But then, why would it be a plant? Plants didn't move of their own volition—*usually*.

Something—not Ivy—hissed, followed by another metallic scraping. *That has to be the trap.*

Alex winced. Hopefully whatever she'd caught wasn't hurt. If it was, no matter how dirty or disagreeable the animal might be, she'd have to take care of it. None of God's creatures deserved to stay in a trap until they died of starvation or dehydration. Alex had no stomach for senseless killing. Except, perhaps, for the one who'd murdered her daughter. But that killing wouldn't be senseless. It would be justice.

The candlelight hit the metal, live animal trap. Beady mouse eyes lifted to Alex's. At least half of it was a mouse. The back half had the curled, sharp tail of a scorpion.

"Hiss!"

Alex gasped, gaped at it a second longer, and raced back to the rope. "Vera! I can hardly believe—we've caught something that might interest you."

"Plant, animal, or insect?"

Alex sneezed. "It's hard to say, but it's definitely not a plant."

Alex couldn't see Vera's shadowed expression, but she heard a smile in her tone.

"Those are the best kind," Vera said.

Words—a human voice?—whispered from the direction of the trap.

Goose bumps trickled down Alex's spine. The creature couldn't talk, could it? She stepped closer to the trap.

Ivy batted at the cage. More important, she glowed. *What makes her do that?*

The creature hissed again.

Alex lunged forward. "Get away from there, Ivy!"

Ivy batted it again, but this time, the creature's tail arched and shot forward. It stung Ivy's paw.

"Meow!" Ivy shrank back from the cage. She licked her paw. She also stopped glowing.

"Ivy! Are you all right?" Alex scooped her into her arms.

Ivy's breathing turned ragged.

Alex hugged her against her chest. She ran her hand along the length of her body. *Ivy! What's happening?*

Ivy's breathing slowed.

Alex raced to the rope. "Vera!" she yelled. "Are you sure that tarantula of yours can heal?"

"That's what his eyes say."

Ivy's muscles relaxed.

Tears filled Alex's eyes, but she blinked them away. "The creature stung Ivy, and Ivy—she's struggling to breathe!." Alex set Ivy inside her closed jacket, but the cat was too limp to hold herself there, so Alex wrapped one arm around her and grabbed hold of the rope. She pulled herself upward, but her grip slipped before her toes left the ground. "I can't carry Ivy and climb at the same time," she called up the shaft.

"Stay there."

Suddenly, Vera's floppy hat dropped down the shaft and plunked to the ground. "Tie the rope around it, and set Ivy inside. I'll pull her up."

Alex blinked hard. She absolutely would not cry.

"Something down there is upset," Vera said. "The luminal vibrations coming out of that cavern feel like thunder."

"If it's that creature that poisoned Ivy, it'll have to stay upset." Alex set Ivy in the hat and wound the rope around it. "Pull!"

The rope tightened, and the hat with Ivy nestled inside moved upward.

Alex steadied the hat until she could no longer reach it. She then folded her arms, hugging herself. *Please be all right. I can't bear another loss.*

"I've got her!" Vera said. "And now—Alistair's on top of her. Oh, my! It's incredible. You should see this, Alex. Alistair ran right to Ivy's paw and bit it."

Alex cringed at the thought of a big, hairy spider biting her pet and glared into the darkness toward the mouse-scorpion. "Ivy better live," she muttered.

The creature hissed, and the trap scraped across the ground.

Alex furrowed her brows. Had that creature understood her? "How is Ivy?" Alex called up to Vera.

"She's still breathing."

Alex went to the trap. The creature had already eaten the grain Alex had left as bait when she'd set the trap, but Alex didn't care. Every inch of her wanted to leave that creature right where it was. Leave it to starve to death. But even as she thought those words, something inside her recoiled. She must not feel, only think. That creature, if it had characteristics similar to common mice or scorpions, was a living being that had acted only out of instinct. She had to do what she could to help it. Yet, how could she do so without getting stung?

"Is Ivy still all right?" Alex called.

"Same as before," Vera dropped the rope back into the shaft. "What about that animal?"

"Also the same. Actually, Vera, when Ivy stabilizes, I need you to find me a long, sturdy stick."

"The creature is too big for your specimen case, I take it."

"It is." Yet, letting that creature loose to run free and perhaps sting Alex the next time she entered the cavern to hunt for the mushrooms seemed foolhardy. But there was nothing else for it. She had to let it loose.

A couple of minutes later, Vera dropped a leafless tree branch about five feet long into the shaft. It landed on the ground next to Alex. She, clutching the rope with one hand, extended the stick toward the trap. Its tip trembled slightly. Still, with careful, deliberate movements, she maneuvered it through the wire mesh and nudged the release lever. The mechanism clicked, and the door swung open.

Alex dropped the stick and jumped up to the closest knot on the rope. She scrambled upward, hand over hand, to the next knot. Hopefully she was high enough above the ground that the creature couldn't reach her.

"Ivy's breathing normally now," Vera said when Alex climbed out of the shaft.

Alex gazed longingly down at the still-unexplored second tunnel and exhaled. "Thank the heavens."

Chapter 2

THE ENCLOSED HANSOM CAB Alex had hired at the Wessen, Massachusetts railway station was much more comfortable than the buckboard wagon she traveled in back in Idaho, but, like her current surroundings, it was also more austere. And constricting. And oh-so-boringly refined.

The driver stopped the cab before Uncle Henry's white mansion at the lane's end. So little had changed in five years since Alex had left the place that she felt suspended between past and present. She could almost smell the Joe Pye weeds and taste the bitter tea she'd once brewed for when Fay had grown sick with fever. Those long-ago summers seemed so impossibly distant . . . so startlingly near. Emotion blurred her eyes. How old had she and Fay been then—sixteen?

"I'll help you out in a moment, Miss," the driver said through the small trap door. He sat on a sprung seat behind and above Alex's compartment.

Alex dabbed her handkerchief to her eyes and forced a smile. It simply wouldn't do for him, or anyone for that matter, to believe she'd lost control of her emotions. "Thank you."

While the driver climbed down from his perch, Alex scooped up Ivy from where she slept on the seat beside her. She placed her inside her carpetbag.

Ivy looked up at Alex.

"Stay quiet for just a little longer," Alex whispered. "Just until the driver's gone."

Ivy yawned, and Alex closed the bag, leaving a small gap at the top to ensure the cat could breathe. Then, gripping it in one gloved hand, Alex climbed out of the hansom cab and waited as the driver unloaded her traveling trunk from the carriage's rear platform. He handed it to her, and soon after, he turned the horse back toward the main road.

Alex, now carrying both cases, strode to the gray stone fence that ran along the front of Uncle Henry's property. She stepped through the black wrought iron gate.

"Metal and rock," she mouthed. "Dissimilar objects forced to stand side by side."

The first time she'd seen that fence and gate, she'd been a newly-orphaned child. She'd just arrived from the West—the farm where she'd grown up. She'd hardly noticed the gate then, but now she suspected Uncle Henry had purposely combined metal and rock to represent life's contrasting elements—hard and soft, rigid and malleable, and especially the old adage that opposites attract. He often did—she bit her lower lip to stop it from quivering—*had done* things like that over the years.

Alex stiffened her spine, walked up the path to the manor's double front doors, and set her luggage down beside her. She pulled a telegram from the curved welt pocket of her dark green linen traveling dress.

The lawyer's message arrived a week and a half ago, the day after her expedition with Vera, and Alex had read and refolded it so often the paper now felt like a worn rag.

> Alexandra Dalton STOP Henry Watson dead STOP Specified you must attend reading of will STOP July twenty-third at 4 PM STOP M Talbot

Alex slid the telegram back into her pocket, closed her eyes, and swallowed. Showing emotion wouldn't restore her uncle back to life, nor would it keep Edna Shaw from fussing over her. Edna Shaw, Uncle Henry's housekeeper, had once been Alex and Fay's ever-doting governess.

Alex tapped the brass door knocker.

Ivy squirmed inside the carpetbag. Alex opened it the rest of the way. "I suppose it's safe enough for you to come out now."

Instead of crawling out, Ivy stood on her hind paws and wrapped her front legs around Alex's shin.

Alex shook her head. The poor thing had been even more clingy since that half-mouse creature had stung her. She was probably afraid she'd run into another one. But then, maybe that wasn't the reason at all. Maybe, as Vera had suggested, Ivy still carried a trace of the creature's poison in her blood. That was bound to make her feel out of sorts.

The front door swung open. Edna, a short, spindly woman with silver hair and astute blue eyes inspected the length of Alex. Edna's gray, tiny-flower-patterned day dress looked just as it had when she'd taught Alex in the upstairs schoolroom, but her apron was as white as a new bolt of cloth. "My dearest girl! Come in."

"Hello, Edna." Alex leaned into Edna's easy embrace and followed her through the front door into the large entry hall. Rather than candles, gas lights now lit the room, but otherwise, very little had changed. The same black walnut floors led to the drawing room on their left, the formal dining room on their right, and directly ahead, a wide staircase flanked by a pale yellow wall with the same crest-patterned bench.

For a moment, Alex wished she, as a child, had dared to slide down the staircase's carved banister from the bedrooms to the basement, defying her Aunt's disapproval. Such a memory would have certainly lifted her spirits.

"I could hardly believe it when your uncle told me you were coming," Edna said. She glanced down at Ivy, who sat on Alex's feet.

"You mean Uncle Henry's lawyer, Mr. Talbot, don't you?" Alex asked.

"Oh, yes, of course. Mr. Talbot."

Alex looked away from Edna—it was easier not to cry that way—and Edna pursed her lips and straightened her apron.

"Forgive me, my child. I didn't mean to upset you."

"I am sad, but it isn't you're fault." Alex scanned the hallway. "Is Fay already here?"

Uncle Henry's daughter would of course inherit the Watson fortune. That was as it should be, but since Uncle Henry had, according to the telegram, specifically asked Alex to be at the reading of his will too, Alex hoped he'd left something to her. A small memento, even a final message would comfort her heart. But even if neither were the case, Alex would have answered her uncle's bidding anyway. Uncle Henry had taken her into his home and family when she was eight after her parents had died of influenza. Alex owed much of the woman she'd become to Uncle Henry. More than that, she'd loved him like her own father.

"I'm afraid you're the first to arrive, my girl." Edna motioned to the drawing room. "If you'll come this way."

Alex furrowed her brows. "Wouldn't this meeting be more appropriate in Uncle Henry's office?"

"His orders were for you to wait in the drawing room."

Alex sighed. Perhaps Mr. Talbot had developed eccentricities in his old age. The heavens knew her uncle had.

"I'll take your bags to your old room for you while you wait." Once again, Edna eyed the length of Alex. "Or would you prefer to freshen up?"

"That's thoughtful of you, but I'll wait until after I've spoken with Mr. Talbot." By then she'd have time to take both a bath and a nap. Alex removed her green walking hat, handed it Edna, and added, "Though, I must ask you to please not open any of my bags."

Edna crooked an eyebrow as if she expected Alex to explain her request, but Alex held her tongue. Not many people, especially a genteel woman, would appreciate finding a specimen jar with a perforated metal lid inside it. Especially one that housed a live tarantula. Vera had insisted Alex take the spider with her in case she needed him to bite Ivy a second time. Alex had suggested they have him bite Ivy right then and be done with it, but Vera had contended that Alistair's powers were untested. It would be better to watch over Ivy and have him bite a second time only if Ivy seemed in danger. In the end, Alex had conceded, promising to keep tabs on Alistair and record any changes in his behavior.

"Instructions noted, Alexandra. As always, your privacy will be respected." Edna, her nose slightly in the air, tucked Alex's hat under her arm, gathered Alex's luggage, and headed to the staircase. "You can find your way, I'm sure."

"Of course." Alex frowned. She'd obviously offended her, but it couldn't be helped. If Vera knew Alistair was there, she'd get rid of him post-haste. Perhaps even destroy him. She had no patience for insects, not even luminal ones.

Alex nudged Ivy off her shoes and moved into the drawing room. She blinked. The tall, framed windows and the long, rectangular mirror beside the back doorway remained the only red elements in the room. Everything else was now white: the tablecloths, chairs, and sofas. Even a delicate off-white carpet had replaced the previous red-and-gold-patterned one. Alex shook her head. What had possessed her uncle to change everything so much? Had he truly not known how important this room had been to Fay and her? Or had it no longer mattered, since both of them had moved away?

She took two slow steps, picturing the nights when she and Fay had been so caught up with their comings and goings that they couldn't sleep. Then, Edna had gathered them there, offered them something warm to drink—tea or hot cocoa—and listened to their hopes and fears. Edna, in turn, had spoken of days she'd wished she'd known: sweet days filled with love and family and children. At those times, Edna had seemed like the mother Alex and Fay wished they still had.

"Hang on to every happiness," Edna would say before Alex and Fay had finally kissed her good night. "Happiness can be fleeting."

Alex fingered the pink ribbon on her wrist. That statement was true enough. Even the happiness she'd once found in that room hadn't lasted. "Come now, Ivy. If I have to sit, you might as well fill my lap."

Ivy mewed, and the two sat on the white velvet wing chair close to the door. Who would arrive next? Fay or Mr. Talbot?

Chapter 3

ABOUT FIFTEEN MINUTES LATER, a sharp rap struck the front door. Hopefully, that was Fay.

Neither Edna nor any of the other servants came to answer it, so Alex set Ivy on the floor and went to do the job. Halfway there, she froze. When she'd first entered the house, she hadn't noticed the small, round mirror next to the entrance. Alex normally didn't take much concern for her reflection, but what she saw shocked her so sharply she couldn't bring herself to look away: her crumpled dress, her wind-strewn hair that looked more like an auburn mop than a fashionable topknot, and especially the dark circles under her green eyes. Was this what happened to a woman who'd spent most of the last week on a train? Or—her stomach hardened—was this what happened to someone who'd lost both her daughter and her husband in one blow? No wonder Edna had suggested she freshen up.

Alex traced the ribbon around her wrist.

Another knock struck the door.

Alex pinched her cheeks to give them a hint of color—it simply wouldn't do for Fay to see her in such a forlorn state. She then gathered Ivy from the floor, knowing the cat would help conceal the wrinkles in her dress, and opened the door.

Her smile disappeared. Her breath—her heart?—stopped. She stared up into the man's hazel eyes. They were the color of a stormy Atlantic sea, surrounded by long, thick lashes tipped with the lightness of his wavy blonde hair. He was tall, straight, and wore the deep charcoal morning coat that had always accentuated the strength and breadth of his arms and shoulders. A man to be reckoned with. Richard Edward Dalton, her estranged husband.

"Hello, luv," he said.

Alex clenched and unclenched the door handle. *What is he doing here?* "Rick."

He quirked a tentative smile. "Can I come in?"

"Why?"

"I've been invited."

Huh? Alex furrowed her brows. Who would invite Rick here? And on the day of the reading of her uncle's will? It couldn't have been her uncle's wishes. Alex had told him how it was Rick's fault that the murderer had taken Mary, and that she'd since cut Rick out of her life. Besides, Richard Dalton was already a man of far greater wealth and prestige than Fay's bank-owning husband could ever hope to achieve. Rick had no need and likely no desire to inherit anything from her uncle. Who then had invited him? Uncle Henry's lawyer, Mr. Talbot?

Of course. Who else could it have been?

"You don't believe me, do you?" Rick continued. "I wondered if you'd require proof." He reached inside his blue vest pocket and pulled out an open telegram. It contained the same message that was written on hers. "As I said, I've been invited."

Alex curled her toes. The first chance she had, she'd chastise Mr. Talbot for even thinking of including Rick in this meeting.

Edna bustled down the stairs. "Come in, Mr. Dalton," she called. "We've been waiting for you."

Which meant Rick had to stay.

Alex, frowning, stiffened her spine and hugged Ivy tighter against her chest. If Alex looked away from Rick, would he believe she felt absolutely nothing at his being there? She didn't know, but it was worth a try.

She turned her head away from him, but before she could test the results of her theory, Rick stepped forward.

Alex moved far enough to the side of the entrance that he couldn't possibly touch her when he walked through the front door. *The front door.* The last time Alex had seen Rick had been in the front doorway of their Southeastern Idaho home. She'd said things. He'd said things. But it wasn't until she'd told him to leave that the color had drained from his face.

"Don't do this, Alex," he'd said. "If I leave, you'll never see me again."

Alex had pressed her hand against her chest and, clenching her blouse, had willed her lips not to tremble. If he didn't leave, how could she look at him without picturing their daughter in his arms? "Please go, Rick."

His pained stare pierced Alex's heart, but rather than reaching for him to comfort him as she once would have done, she dropped her gaze to the floor. He had to leave—for a while—otherwise she'd never learn to live with the grief.

She had heard him catch his breath. She'd watched his feet storm past her and across their front yard to their carriage outside the front gate. But it wasn't until she had lifted her head and watched the carriage disappear from her sight that the foolishness of what she'd just done—said—had sunk through her. Rick Dalton had not looked back, and Rick Dalton had always been a man of his word; he would not return.

"Now—" Edna's voice brought Alex back to the present. "—will the two of you please follow me upstairs?"

"Why upstairs?" Alex said. "That makes even less sense than meeting in the drawing room."

"It's simply the way it's to be," Edna said.

Rick, standing just inside the doorway, appraised the space between Alex and Edna. Then, with unhurried ease, he held Alex's gaze for a long moment before stepping farther into the foyer. As he passed her, his hand wisped so quickly and close to hers that they almost touched. *Almost*.

Alex bristled. She sidled even farther away from him and placed her hands on her hips. "You aren't surprised to see me," she told him. "Why?"

The corners of his lips nudged upward, but his incessant gaze clung to hers. What could it mean? He'd never looked at her like that when they were together. Did he, perhaps, want something from her?

"I expected you'd be here," he answered simply. "Your uncle is, I mean *was*, important to you." He leaned his walking cane against the door frame, set his top hat on the nearby hat rack, and headed for the staircase.

Alex, not to be outdone, shifted Ivy to her other arm and hurried past Rick and up the stairs to Edna. She grabbed Edna's elbow. "Shouldn't we wait for Fay?"

"It's good of you to concern yourself, my girl," Edna said, "but I have my instructions. This way, please."

Alex narrowed her gaze, rubbed the back of her neck, and peered back and forth between Edna and Rick. What was going on?

Neither Rick nor Edna seemed to notice her consternation. They only continued on, with Edna leading the way and Rick following Alex. The three ascended the staircase to the second floor. All of the manor's bedrooms lined both sides of the long hallway.

Edna passed the guest chamber and stopped in front of Fay's old room. It was across from Alex's. "This will be your room, Mr. Dalton. I can have one of the servants bring up your luggage if you'd like."

Alex flinched, and her mouth soured. "He's staying here! Whatever for?"

"For as long as he's needed," Edna said.

"Needed for what?" Ivy squirmed within Alex's too-tight embrace, and Alex relaxed her grip. "What aren't you telling me?"

Edna pursed her lips into a tight frown, but Rick stepped in beside Alex and leaned close enough their elbows touched. "Patience, my—Alex," he whispered, "All is not what it seems." He looked at Edna. "I left my suitcase outside on the front stairs."

"Very good, sir." Edna motioned for them to continue following her down the hall.

Alex folded her arms tighter around Ivy. She stepped quicker, hoping the heated feel of Rick's presence next to her would dissipate, but instead, it grew stronger. Any minute now, she told herself, Rick would be the self-assured man she'd always known him to be. The man who hated to be beholden to anyone. The man who wouldn't want to be near her any more than she wanted to be near him and would therefore decline staying in her uncle's house.

But he remained silent.

Alex stumbled—not enough to fall, and Rick caught her upper arm. He steadied her then quickly released her.

Swallowing, Alex petted Ivy. At the same time, Rick cleared his throat and straightened the knotted scarf at his neck. Neither spoke, but the air around them thickened.

Edna knocked on Uncle Henry's bedchamber door.

Alex, coming back to herself, backstepped. Emotion flooded through her. She couldn't go in there, wouldn't go in there. The last time she'd seen Uncle Henry, he'd been well and full of life, and he'd been in that room. Knowing Edna, the room would now be in order and much of her uncle's belongings would have already been packed away. But right then, to see those walls, that floor, and perhaps even his bed felt like walking into an abyss.

She blinked back the tears that filled her eyes. "I can't do this."

Rick wrapped his arm around her shoulders. He hugged her against his side. "No need to worry, luv," he whispered. "You'll see Uncle Henry again."

Alex sniffled, and Rick nodded to Edna.

Edna opened the door.

Chapter 4

ALEX AND RICK STEPPED into Uncle Henry's bedchamber. Alex shaded her eyes from the late afternoon sunlight streaming through the western window and gazed at the canopied bed. Between two Thomas Birch paintings of ships battling a frantic sea, the bed stood like a silent beacon—

"It's good to see you, Alex."

Alex did a double take. A white-haired man, his face creased with more wrinkles than she remembered, lay upright in the bed with his head propped against a stack of pillows. "Uncle Henry!" She blinked, peered at Edna and Rick, and blinked again. "You're alive."

"Obviously."

"But I thought—Mr. Talbot's telegram said you were dead!"

"As you see, I am not. I told Talbot to send that message."

Alex's muscles quivered—in anger or relief, she didn't know—but she balled her hands into fists. "What are you saying?" She again glimpsed over at Edna, who winced, and at Rick, who folded his arms across his chest. "I don't understand," she said to Uncle Henry. "Why would you do this?"

"Isn't it obvious? I needed to get you here, and this seemed the simplest solution."

Alex forced herself to breathe. She shook her head and back-stepped until she bumped into the bureau behind her. "How could you manipulate me like that? I've been grieving ever since I received the telegram. I thought I'd never see you again."

Rick, beside her, growled softly.

Uncle Henry frowned. "Perhaps this isn't one of my prouder moments, but I'm satisfied with the result. I knew you'd be too focused on your work in the West to come for a less imperative reason."

"You were wrong! I'd do anything I could for you."

"Would you?" He gave Rick a measured nod, and Rick, in response, glanced at Alex and walked toward the window.

"Wait a minute, Rick!" Alex gripped the carved wooden handle of one of the bureau's drawers. "You knew Uncle Henry was alive?"

Rick turned back to her. "I did."

"How could you—how could either of you—let me grieve like that?"

"It was the last thing I wanted to do," Rick said, "but—"

"Now, now." Edna walked up behind Alex and patted her upper arm. "Let's not quibble."

Alex shrugged out of her grip. "Unlike some people around here," she added, "I can't—won't—just up and forsake my responsibilities for no good reason."

Rick's gaze wavered, and a sudden emptiness filled Alex's heart. Why hadn't she shot that barb at Uncle Henry, the real culprit? She'd promised herself most faithfully that if she ever saw Rick again, she wouldn't throw it at him a second time. It was cruel, and she didn't want to be cruel. Yet there she was, throwing it at him anyway. Because he had known about her uncle and she hadn't. Because she'd mourned for no reason. Because she felt foolish. Because—because there was none of the hurt in Rick's expression that she felt roiling inside her, and he should feel hurt. Their daughter had been murdered because of his irresponsible, reckless, ever-distracted ways, and he had left Alex to deal with her broken heart alone. He knew her well enough to know she hadn't really wanted him to leave, that she'd said those things only because she needed to get them out of her system. But he'd left anyway, which meant he'd wanted to leave—to run away from her and their lives together.

Uncle Henry lifted his hand, palm outward. "Hold on there, girl. I deserve your ire, but Rick and Edna were only following my instructions."

"How could you, Rick? Knowing everything I'd—we'd—just gone through with Mary?"

He reached out for her, but she moved back from him. Rick lowered his arm. "I did tell him that, luv. That it wouldn't be right to put your heart through so much pain again, but—"

"But I convinced him otherwise," Uncle Henry cut in. "This is my doing. Not his."

Alex glared between him and Rick. Even if she did feel a bit lighter inside because her uncle was alive, she didn't have to let them know that. Not yet. "Why am I here?" she asked Uncle Henry.

Uncle Henry ran his hand over his mouth, and all at once, worry niggled at the back of Alex's mind. She strode to the bed, stopped next to his side, and glared down at him. "And why are you in bed so late in the afternoon? Surely your scheme didn't require this."

Uncle Henry shifted taller. He held her gaze. "I'm not dead, but I am dying."

Alex stared at him. His wrinkled face was paler than she'd first noticed, blue rimmed his eye sockets, and though his lips turned upward in a slight smile, she saw no joy, only resignation. "Please don't, Uncle. If it's not the truth—please don't."

"It is the truth."

Alex felt the blood drain from her face. From dead to alive to dying? She bit her lower lip to keep it from trembling.

A firm though gentle hand settled on Alex's right shoulder, and calm flashed through her. *Rick.*

She stiffened, stepped away from him, and set Ivy on the floor. How dare he use his touch to settle her nerves now? He'd backed away from her when the sheriff had told them they'd found Mary's body. He should have held her then. Cried with her. Not left.

"He only has a few weeks," Rick said. "That's why I gave into his wishes."

Uncle Henry frowned. "That will be all, Edna."

"Very good, Sir. Ring if you need anything."

Alex watched Edna leave. Watched the door click softly closed behind her.

"Time to get down to business," Uncle Henry said. "Sit next to me, both of you."

Alex perched on the bed's edge near her uncle's knees, with Rick standing beside her. His long eyelashes shadowed his gaze, which remained fixed on Uncle Henry.

"No, I don't know why I'm here," Rick said to Alex under his breath.

Ivy skirted round Alex's ankles.

"How did you know that's what I was going to ask you?" Alex said.

"I lived with you for five years." Finally, he turned to her. "I know your expressions."

And still you left.

Uncle Henry's eyes brightened. "Just as I thought the moment I introduced the two of you: you're quite suited for each other."

Alex pressed her lips together even though her cheeks burned. *Look at Uncle Henry. Only at Uncle Henry.*

Rick cleared his throat. "Tell us why you've brought us here, Sir."

"Very well." Uncle Henry looked straight at Alex. "Before I die, I want the two of you to find out who killed my Pauline."

Cold settled in the base of Alex's stomach. She blinked. "You still believe she was murdered? I thought you gave up on that notion years ago."

Ivy jumped into Alex's lap.

"Then you don't know me as well as I thought you did. The Night Hag is a legend, not a murderer."

Alex set her hand over top of Uncle Henry's where it rested on the brown comforter covering him. "You could have asked me for my help years ago, as you did with some of your other cases."

Uncle Henry lifted an eyebrow.

She frowned. "I mean puzzles." Uncle Henry was a businessman, not a detective, but he loved analyzing facts and rearranging them into something that made sense. His policeman friend, Captain Sutter, knew that about him and had allowed him to look into their unsolved cases. Uncle Henry's work wasn't officially approved, but since the police caught several criminals because of his "puzzling," the judicial system turned a blind eye. "You said I was good at solving cases," Alex added.

"You are. And we did unravel several perplexing puzzles. But your aunt's death was too upsetting for you—for all of us. At the time, I felt it best to keep you and your cousin from it. I still would if things were different."

If you weren't dying. Alex bit the inside of her cheeks. She would not lose control of her emotions. Not in front of her Uncle, and especially not in front of Rick.

"Until a few weeks ago, I thought I knew how and by whom Pauline had been killed," Uncle Henry continued, "but I couldn't prove it to the police's satisfaction. Without proof, as you well know, the police could do nothing to the man. I kept track of him, though, so I'd know where to send the authorities once I uncovered the necessary evidence."

"Apparently something changed your mind about your suspect," Rick said.

Uncle Henry took the half-filled water glass from the end table next to his bed and drank two small sips. "The man died last year of natural causes. I thought he'd gotten away with murder. But a few weeks ago, one of my bank clerks, Jeremiah Godfrey, died under circumstances similar to Pauline's death, and once again, the authorities officially listed it as unexplained."

"But unofficially?" Rick said.

Uncle Henry narrowed his eyes. "The Night Hag."

Alex drew her eyebrows together and slowly ran her hand across the length of Ivy's back. When it had first been noised about the community that the Night Hag had killed her aunt, Uncle Henry had explained the legend to her and Fay. The Night Hag was the ghost of a dead witch who attacked victims during their nightmares, sitting on their chests until they either smothered or died of fright. Alex hadn't heard anything of the Night Hag since then. Was this just another local ghost story being circulated?

"More superstitious neighbors?" she asked.

"Yes. But also Godfrey's young son."

"What other similarities were there? I assume you pointed them out to Captain Sutter?"

Uncle Henry grinned.

"What?" she said.

"You haven't changed much, Alexandra Blake."

Alex smiled at his use of her full maiden name. It felt like a subtle compliment, and for a moment, everything seemed as right and well in their world as it had ever been. "What were the similarities? The deaths were what—eleven years apart?"

"Both victims felt sick earlier in the day and both cried out in the night before they died."

Alex frowned. She glanced up at Rick. Was Uncle Henry serious? "Those are the only similarities? No wonder the police think a connection between them is a stretch."

"Yes."

Ivy jumped from Alex's lap and walked across the room to the fireplace.

Rick cleared his throat. "You're not asking us to hunt a demon, are you, Sir?"

"I have never believed and never will believe a supernatural being intruded on my wife's sleep in the middle of the night and squeezed the life out of her."

"I don't believe that either," Alex said. "But I did think she was sick, and I don't recall illness being related to the Night Hag legend."

"It isn't. Which, as I said, is one of the similarities between the two cases."

Alex stood. She ran her hand up and down her arm and paced to the solid mahogany door. Though very few sounds slipped through it, there had been a few nights she and Fay had locked themselves in one of their rooms so they wouldn't hear Uncle Henry and Aunt Pauline arguing.

"You'd be better off hiring professional investigators," Alex said.

"I already have, several times, but each learned nothing more than I already knew."

Alex returned to his bedside.

Uncle Henry took Alex's hand in one of his and Rick's in the other. "This is the last request I'll ever make of either of you. Please find my wife's murderer."

Alex and Rick looked at each other.

"You still can't see what a force the two of you are together, can you?" Uncle Henry added.

Alex groaned, kept her face fully averted from Rick's, and pulled back from her uncle, but he held her fast.

"Is that what this is really about?" she said. "Getting us back together?"

"In part," Uncle Henry said, "because, whether or not you realize it, you're still in love with each other."

"We never were in love," Alex said. "We were only friends. Tell him, Rick."

Rick said nothing. Couldn't he even support her in that?

Uncle Henry released them and briefly lifted his right hand. "I meant what I said. You have adventurous hearts, are internally driven, and see facts in nonstandard ways. Rick also has the means, intelligence, and"—He looked at Rick, who shook his head slightly—"and physical prowess to accomplish whatever has to be done. You, Alex, have an uncanny intuition and an ultra-sensitivity to luminal elements that I've come to rely on. Apart, you're magnificent. Together, you're unstoppable."

Alex crossed her right arm in front of her waist and pressed her left fingertips to her temple. It had been ages since she'd eaten a fresh lemon, but right then the memory of its sour, stinging taste puckered the inside of her mouth. "You want me to work with Rick?"

"I do."

"You've studied this case for years and come up empty. What if we do too?"

"I wouldn't ask you if I thought that could happen."

She pursed her lips and walked to the window. Though its square glass panes seemingly divided the yard into sections of full-leafed trees, red bushes, and multi-shaped flowers, they also revealed a unified picture. Would her life always be like that? Broken until someone else told her how the pieces fit together?

Not if I connect them my way first. She rubbed the back of her neck and once again faced her uncle. "I will look into it for a few days, but after that, I have to get back home." *And figure out who killed Mary. And why.*

Rick glanced at Alex's fingers, the ribbon on her wrist, her eyes. His gaze softened. "Don't you want to stay until—the end?"

The emotion she'd held back welled in her eyes. Why did he say that? Couldn't he see how hard she was trying to keep her feelings in check? But then, maybe he was too obsessed with who knew what to notice anything except what was going on inside his own mind.

Alex looked back at her uncle. "You said Aunt Pauline and this Jeremiah Godfrey were sick the days they died. Did anyone discover from what?"

"No one knew. I didn't even know Pauline was anything more than out of sorts until Edna mentioned it."

Alex held her uncle's gaze. All the days she'd known him, his blue eyes had appeared clear, composed, and more determined than she'd sometimes liked, but now they also held vulnerability.

"You'll find a file labeled 'Pauline' in the top right drawer of my office desk," he added.

Rick sauntered to Alex's side. To his credit, when his elbow bumped her upper arm, he sidestepped another foot away. It was a much more respectable distance for a not-quite husband to stand next to his not-quite wife. Of course it was.

"Do you have a file for Mr. Godfrey as well?" Rick asked.

"A small one," Uncle Henry replied. "I'll contact Captain Sutter. He may have more information."

"It's too late in the day to reach him now," Alex said.

"Tomorrow then." Uncle Henry sighed, leaned his head against his pillow, and closed his eyes. "The one thing we have that the police don't is Mr. Godfrey's ten-year-old son. I'd already noted the similarities in Jeremiah's and Pauline's cases and wanted to speak with the boy anyway, so I made the necessary arrangements for him to stay here until the authorities could find his relatives. His name is Louis. Edna has settled him in the children's room. I have questioned him, and he's most affable, but all I've ascertained, as I said before, is he believes the Night Hag killed his father. Perhaps the two of you will get better answers."

Alex shoved a strand of her hair behind her ear. Her uncle had behaved most generously when he and Pauline had taken her into their home, but after Aunt Pauline had died, leaving him alone with two girls to care for, Alex had assumed he would come to regret his decision. Not that he'd ever shown any such remorse—he was too much of a gentleman for that—but she'd seen enough of her own father's outbursts to know that for a grown man to be saddled with two dependent girls was more than most could bear, nanny or not. Yet he hadn't sent Alex away. He'd raised her as his own daughter—loved her even. She had no other choice but to help him with his last request.

Alex kissed her uncle on the forehead. "Thank you for everything."

"You'll help me?"

"I will."

Out of the corner of her eye, she saw Rick smile. Maybe he thought they were heading into some grand adventure. If so, he'd likely be disappointed. Investigating crimes was often quite sedentary.

But then, she'd never investigated a Night Hag murder before.

Chapter 5

A LEX STEPPED INTO THE hallway, and Rick, moving in next to her, closed Uncle Henry's bedroom door behind them.

"I'm sorry about all this, Alex," he said. "If I'd seen any other way, I'd have taken it."

Alex scooped Ivy into her arms. How long would it be before she could return home and put this life—Rick—behind her? "I'm surprised you showed up at all. Don't you have a treasure to find?"

"I'm hurt." He pressed his hand over his chest in mock sorrow, but his smile wavered. He was teasing her, yet something about the downward creases around his eyes and the hollowness in his expression told her he meant exactly what he'd said. She had hurt him. She hadn't thought it was possible.

"It's not like I can't get away from my work if I need to," he added. "My partners can search while I'm gone."

"You didn't find it so easy to get away in the past." Alex stepped in the middle of the long beige carpet than ran the length of the hallway.

As a girl, its green mosaics of domes entwined with circles had represented the home she'd found at Watson manor even though it was so different from the farming world she'd grown up in. Today the green meant nausea. And shock. And a coil of emotions she didn't know how to unravel. "Just say it, Rick. What you mean is your treasure is somewhere close."

"No, luv." He grabbed her arm, stopping her.

"Don't call me that."

His expression drooped, and he released her. "The treasure's in New York. I'm here because I promised your uncle I'd help him. And because—because I wanted to be here with you. Can you not see that?"

Familiar warmth flowed through her arm from where he touched her and across the length and breadth of her body. Rick's touch. His comfort. She had missed them. But she hadn't missed the sudden, distant look in his eyes. She knew that expression well. She slid from his grasp and pulled Ivy closer. Her purr thrummed against Alex's chest like a hypnotic pulse. Would Ivy's calming touch someday replace Rick's? "I know it's true that you only do what you want to do, but in this case, I can't understand why you're doing it. Uncle Henry can't mean that much to you."

"You'd be surprised." He swallowed, straightened his lapel, and cleared his throat. He glanced at her out of the corner of his eye. "How are you, Alex? You're doing well, I hope?"

Polite conversation. It might be a poor substitute for the life she and Rick had once shared together, but what more could there be? *Nothing!* She pursed her lips and started toward the children's room at the end of the hall. "I'm doing quite well, if you really want to know. I have a tenant. A fellow mystiobiologist, actually. We work together."

"Vera," he muttered.

Alex froze. She slowly turned and glared at him. "What did you say?"

He paled. "Nothing."

"How do you know my tenant's name?"

"I don't. I mean, I didn't say anything."

She narrowed her eyes. "Have you been spying on me?"

"Of course not." Rick strode ahead of her. "Come along. We don't want to keep Louis past dinnertime. When I was a kid, dinner was the best part of the day, and—" He took a deep breath. "—I smell roast beef."

Alex grabbed his forearm, pulled him around so he faced her, and stared at him. "What do you know about Vera?"

Rick's irises wavered. "We may not be living together, Alex, but you're still my wife. I took an oath to care for you."

Coldness poured through Alex's chest. Rick's parents were from England's upper class and had raised him with America's elite. He knew whom to contact, and he could charm a snake out of its dinner. It would be nothing for him to have found Alex such a perfect companion. Why, oh why, hadn't she recognized that when Vera, a woman with money who also wanted to live and work with her, had suddenly shown up on Alex's doorstep. Why hadn't she seen it was all too good to be true?

Alex bit her lip. Because she'd been desperate and had needed a miracle. "You sent Vera to live with me, didn't you?" She spoke loudly so her voice wouldn't shake.

"Define *sent*."

"How could you, Rick?" She glared at him, lifted her hand, palm forward, in front of her, and stormed down the hall. *Of all the condescending . . .* She'd thought she'd finally taken a step toward financial independence, but all along she'd been a pawn in another one of his machinations.

Rick rushed after her. He grabbed her arm. "All right. I did hire her. But it's not what you think."

"Oh no? I think you paid Vera a lot of money so she could pay me and I would think I was supporting myself."

"All right. It is what you think. But you were struggling to make ends meet, and you wouldn't accept the money I sent you."

Alex yanked her arm away from him. "I can take care of myself, Rick."

"I know you can. Your independence is one of the things I love about you. But when I met Vera and learned she has the same interests you have . . ." He shrugged. "I'd considered her an answer to my prayers."

"What prayers? That you'd find a way to spy on me?"

"That I'd find a way to comfort your heart."

Alex's throat constricted. So many times she'd wished for comfort too. Hungered for the touch of Mary's hand and the warmth of her smile. And yes, even dreamed of the peace she'd felt when the three of them had lived together as a once-complete family. But those yearnings were always shadowed by the reality of the bread she'd rationed so she could eat one more day, the hot water she'd drunk instead of tea, the blankets she'd piled on her bed because she had too little wood for her stove, and most of all, the empty, silent house. All because of Rick.

She scowled at him. "I'd have made it somehow."

Rick inched so close she could hear his breath swelling in and out in rhythm with his chest. Energy pulsed between them. "I know you would have," he said softly. "You're strong and smart. But don't suffer if you don't have to. Please?"

She stepped back, not as far away as he'd moved toward her but enough she could breathe without feeling that at any moment he might take her into his arms and force away her loneliness. Which she absolutely didn't want him to do.

"I'm sorry about Mary. About everything," he continued. "If I could take back that day, I would. You must know that, must know how much I, like you, loved—love—our Mary."

He took Alex's hand again, and this time when the comforting warmth spread through her, she didn't have the strength to pull it away. Her body craved peace.

"Please, Alex," he said. "There must be some way we can get past what's happened to us. Please forgive me."

Alex closed her eyes. She pictured how Rick and she used to be: their easy familiarity with each other, their laughter, their joint luminal and treasure-hunting escapades. Her ribs clenched around her lungs. *You were supposed to be watching Mary, not studying a stupid treasure map!*

"Please forgive me," he said again.

Hateful words she'd repeated so many times they felt like a broken part of her leapt to the tip of her tongue, but when she opened her mouth to say them, they died on her lips. Rick was not only Mary's father, but he had also been Alex's best friend. She knew his expressions as well as she knew the freckle on the back of her hand, and right then his eyes looked as empty as her heart felt. Was it right for her to continue to punish him? What if she had been the one that had looked away—at a luminal plant, perhaps—when Mary had been taken? How long could she have borne the guilt?

But then, she wouldn't have looked away. Still, she said, "I'm sorry too, Rick."

"Thank you." He pulled her toward him, but she backed out of his grip and shook her head.

"I can't," she said. "You know as well as I do that our marriage was based more on trust than anything else, and now we don't even have that."

His eyes glazed. "That's not true for me, Alex."

"It is for me." She set Ivy on the floor, waited while the cat licked her paw, and again headed down the hall. Their footsteps—hers, Rick's, Ivy's—plodded softly over the carpet.

Rick walked beside Alex. His arm bumped hers. He tensed stepped away. The veins on his hands protruded as he clenched and un-clenched his hands. "When I last spoke with Vera, she said you were looking for a plant you hoped might help you learn more about Mary's killer. Have you found it?"

"Not yet."

They reached the children's room. Alex clasped the brass door-knob, and Rick's warm, comforting hand rested on hers. "Let's figure these deaths out for your uncle, but after that, I want to help you find the one who murdered our Mary."

Alex turned to him. Again, his face was so close to hers that if she bowed her head, even just an inch, her forehead would bump his lips. "You want to help me?"

"Always."

Alex took a deep breath and turned away from him. She stared so hard at the door that for a moment the mahogany knots and grains represented worlds and stars joined by crooked roads. What did Rick mean by *always*? Leaving her to bear her grief alone in the wake of Mary's death was not the same as helping her *always*—even if she had told him to leave.

She stood taller. Whatever it meant, wherever it led, she understood him enough to know he believed what he said, at least for now. She would believe him, but she must also tread carefully. "When we question Louis, I think we should concentrate on finding more details about his father. And about the night he died. Maybe there's something more that connects him and Aunt Pauline."

"All right, yes, but I also want to know why Louis believes the Night Hag killed his father."

She rolled her eyes. "This is serious, Rick."

He grinned and released her hand, but he didn't step back from her. "I am serious. We need to compare it to the testimonies of those who thought the same thing about your aunt. I won't let you down, luv."

She closed her eyes, braced her emotions, and turned the doorknob. "I told you not to call me that."

He exhaled, but said nothing until they'd stepped into the children's room. He closed the door before Ivy could follow them inside. "You're coddling that cat too much."

"This from the man who hired Vera."

"That's different. I'm not keeping you under my control. I'm just helping."

Alex pursed her lips and pressed her tongue over her top teeth. "You don't know what Ivy's been through."

"What has she—" Rick narrowed his gaze. He stared at Alex. "Maybe what I should ask is, what have *you* been through?"

Ivy scratched the other side of the door. Alex opened it and picked her up. "I said I'm fine."

Chapter 6

L OUIS GODFREY JUMPED UP from the desk and backed into the far right corner of the room. He folded his too-thin arms and shook his long, brown bangs out of his face. He quick-glanced between Rick, Alex, and the door.

"Hello, Louis," Alex said. "I'm Mrs. Dalton, Mr. Watson's niece, and this is Mr. Dalton, my husband."

Louis swallowed.

"But you can call me Alex." Society frowned upon children calling their elders by their first names, but the moment Edna had insisted on that familiarity between her, Alex, and Fay, the three of them had developed a friendly, trusting relationship. Would the same technique work with Louis?

"And call me Rick," Rick added.

The tendons in Louis's neck strained the way Ivy's muscles had when she'd faced the mouse-scorpion creature, and emotion scorched the back of Alex's sinuses. *Fear.* Had Mary been afraid before she'd died? Had she believed her parents had forsaken her?

Alex blinked those thoughts away and turned to Rick, giving her a moment to slow her heartbeat. "Wait here," she mouthed to him. "We don't want to scare him."

"Maybe too late," he mouthed in return.

Alex looked back to the boy and smiled softly. She moved across the red rug with its gold geometric pattern, remembering how Aunt Pauline would often enter their childhood room and ask, "See how important mathematics is?"

Alex crouched in front of Louis. "I'm Alexandra Dalton. Mr. Watson is my uncle. I used to live here when I was a young girl." She pointed to the bureau in the far left corner. "My cousin and I kept our dolls in those drawers. We pretended they were the dolls' secret hideaways."

Louis, his eyes wide, stared at her but said nothing.

"We'd put them there and playact like we couldn't find them." Alex said. "Do you do that too? Pretend like toys are alive?"

"Toys are for babies."

Alex swallowed. Louis's expression seemed to close off even more, but at least he'd spoken. "You're right, of course. You're obviously much more grown up than we were in those days."

He, frowning, turned away from her, and with his arms still folded, leaned his side against the wall behind him.

"Of course he was more grown up." Rick nodded to Alex, indicating for her to let him try talking with the boy, and angled away from him and sauntered toward the nearby desk. He motioned to the note paper on top of it. "Looks like Edna's already given you school assignments."

"Mathematics," Louis grumbled.

Alex smiled. *Rick's charm is working.*

Rick gave Alex a quick nod and inched toward Louis. "I was never overly fond of school, but I did like mathematics. Not the same with you?"

"I detest it."

"Really?" Rick continued. "All those sums, divisions, and even the multiplications were challenges I couldn't wait to solve."

Something about Rick's words seemed to catch Louis attention, for the boy's rigid posture softened. He uncrossed his arms and drummed his fingers—just once—against his leg.

Tread carefully.

Alex bit the inside of her lower lip and moved to Rick's side. She picked up the note paper, perused it, and set it back down. "Goodness," she said to Rick. "I'm glad someone like's mathematics, but it was much too difficult for me. Is that why math distresses you too, Louis? Because it's difficult?"

Louis gave a slight nod. "I can't bear getting the answers wrong."

"Which I always did," Alex continued. "And then I'd have to do them again."

"Punishment," Louis spat under his breath.

Punishment? Repeating the math problems was the only punishment Edna had ever given her and Fay. But then . . . maybe he wasn't talking about Edna.

Once again, Alex turned back to Louis. "Math is definitely difficult, but so are a lot of other things in life, aren't they."

Louis looked at her and glanced away.

"Like right now, Rick and I are trying to figure out how my aunt died. That's a really difficult puzzle for us to solve." She glanced at Rick, and he gave her a slight nod. "We don't want to make things harder for you, Louis," she continued, "but would it be alright if we ask you a few questions about your father's death? My uncle thinks you might know something that can help us figure out how my aunt died."

"All I knows is the Night Hag killed him."

"What makes you believe that?" Rick asked.

"He—he yelled out. In the night. That's what happens."

Alex tilted her head. "Did you check on him when he yelled? Did you see anyone else in the room?"

The boy flinched and pressed himself tighter into the corner. He lifted his chin. "I didn't go to his room."

"Why not?"

"He didn't call for me."

Alex took another forward step, but before she'd taken a second, Rick gave her a small shake of his head. Alex held his gaze. Rick had always been good at reading people. She would follow his instincts.

"What else can you tell us about the day your father died?" she asked Louis.

"He wasn't my father. He just told people that. My mother left me at a convent when I was a baby. Later, Mr. Godfrey and his missus got me from the orphanage."

"Did they adopt you?" Alex said.

"It wasn't like that with them."

Louis's glare seemed more a challenge than an admission of truth. Was he lying?

Rick touched Alex's arm and inched closer to Louis. He stopped about four feet from him.

Louis hunched his shoulders.

"Can you tell us what you remember about the day he died?" Rick said.

Louis shrugged. "I only saw him a couple of times."

"Once at breakfast, maybe?" Rick added.

Louis nodded.

"What time was that?" Alex asked.

"He leaves for work at eight, so before then."

"What did you do after he went to work? Go to school?"

"Not in the summer."

"Of course." Alex frowned. "Who else was with you?"

"I'm not a baby. I can take care of myself."

"With Jeremiah's wife gone, what else was the man supposed to do?" Rick cut in. "He had to make a living. And Louis is old enough he may have had his own job."

"I had chores," Louis said.

Alex scanned Louis's thin frame, red and calloused hands, and the dark circles under his eyes. Had Jeremiah provided the boy with more work than nourishment?

"So the next time you saw Mr. Godfrey was when?" Rick asked. "At dinner?"

"At the baseball game. He was an outfielder."

Alex half smiled. In past years, she'd attended a few community baseball games with Fay and Uncle Henry. Businessmen and charity workers had set up so many activity and refreshment booths near the event it was paramount to a fair. "Did his team win?"

"I don't know. I went for the food. But I expect so. He was happy when he got home."

"So you saw him after the game," Rick said.

"From my bedroom window. I stayed in my room."

Rick glanced at Alex.

"But you saw him well enough to know he was happy?" Alex said.

Louis flipped his hair out of his eyes again. "No. I mean—I heard him, all right? He was whistling when he came in the house. He always whistled when he got what he wanted."

"Do you know what time that was?" Alex asked.

"Prob'ly about five. I got home from the game at four."

"We heard Mr. Godfrey was sick that day. Do you know if that's true?"

Louis shrugged.

"What about at breakfast?" Rick said. "How did he seem then?"

"Cross—same as always."

"Not sick?"

Another shrug. "Can I get back to my studies now? Miss Edna said I had to finish before dinner."

"I have only one more question," Rick said. "Is there any reason, other than that you heard Mr. Godfrey holler, that makes you believe the Night Hag killed him?"

Louis clenched the upper rim of the straight-backed desk chair so tightly his knuckles turned white. His lower lip quivered. "I didn't see a ghost or witch, if that's what you mean."

Alex narrowed her eyes. Though Louis's face had paled, he didn't cower. If anything, he stood taller. Defiant, even. Louis might not have seen a ghost, but something had upset him. Something he obviously did not want to reveal.

Rick set his hand on Alex's shoulder, but he spoke to Louis. "Do you mind if the two of us take a look around your house?"

"It's none of my care."

"Would you like to go with us?" Alex said. "I doubt anyone knows the way around it better than you do."

"I'll never go there again."

Alex clamped her left hand over Mary's pink ribbon. When the sheriff had told her and Rick the police had found Mary's body in the grass by the river, she'd vowed never to go there either. Some places, like people, were too hard to face more than once. Yet, ultimately, she had returned to hunt for clues.

Someone tapped on the door.

Rick opened it.

Edna stood in the doorway. She carried a pair of black pressed pants and a white shirt over her bent arm. She smiled apologetically at Alex and looked to Louis. "Cook says it's almost time for dinner. Have you finished your studies?"

"Not yet."

"That's our fault," Rick said.

Edna handed Louis the clothes. "I expected these two would mess up your schedule. All right, we won't worry about mathematics tonight. Come down to dinner as soon as you've dressed." She looked to Alex and Rick. "The two of you will be joining Louis, of course?"

"We'll be there," Alex said, "but if we're late, have him start without us."

"Very well."

Alex and Rick followed Edna from the room, but while Edna continued down the hall to the stairway, Alex paused.

Rick cupped her elbow. "What do you have in mind? It's too late in the evening to inspect the Godfrey home now."

"We'll go in the morning. But I think we should record what we've just learned from Louis. We don't want to forget anything."

"There isn't much to forget."

"So it shouldn't take us very long."

"Still meticulous." He placed his hand on her shoulder. "It's another of the things I love about you, Alex. And miss."

Alex's muscles relaxed, but she looked decidedly away from him. If he saw the emotion welling behind her eyes, he might misinterpret her feelings as meaning she felt something more for him than they did. And the fact was, she didn't know what it meant, what she felt, what she wanted to feel. She knew only that deep inside her heart, she still hurt.

Chapter 7

Like Alex had noted in the entry hall, Uncle Henry's office was exactly as she'd remembered it: dark mahogany floors, wood paneled walls, and the large desk that spanned the center of the far side of the room. Alex and her uncle had spent hours together at that desk, studying reference books and going over lists of facts they'd written on the chalkboard. But her favorite part of those days was how they'd thrown theories back and forth as quickly as the firelight flickered from the candelabra hanging from the high ceiling above it. She'd loved those days, and though she hadn't ultimately embraced criminal detective work the way her uncle had encouraged her to do, she had developed keen analytical instincts that well served her work as a mystiobiologist.

Alex sat in her uncle's leather chair, recorded the short list of facts Louis had given them about Mr. Godfrey's death, and finally slid the paper to the middle of the desk. Ivy, sitting in her lap, meowed.

"If this doesn't suit you," Alex said to her, "jump down. Prove to me you're well again."

Ivy licked her paw.

Rick draped his morning coat on the back of the chair next to Alex and sat in it.

Ivy hissed at him.

"What's Ivy upset about?" Rick rolled his white shirt sleeves up to his elbows.

Alex dragged her gaze from his forearm. "I'm assuming it's because a luminal creature stung her with its scorpion tail."

"Poor thing." Rick reached to pet Ivy's head, but Ivy slunk back from him. "She still doesn't like me, does she?"

"I don't think she liked you kicking her out of your bed."

"She's still mad about that?"

"You offended her."

He harrumphed. "I'm sorry she's still angry, but I'm not sorry I did it. I liked someone else there better."

Heat rose to Alex's cheeks. *Their bed. Rick's arms around her . . . her face nuzzled against his chest . . . his lips against the top of her head* . . . She cleared her throat. How could she keep a clear head—make correct decisions—if she let her mind wander like that?

"Besides," Rick added, "I'm not particularly fond of waking up with a cat's tail on my face."

She turned away from him, so he wouldn't see her smile over her memory of his black and orange "mustache."

"That hardly matters," Alex said. "Ivy didn't like you much before then, either." She retrieved the files on Aunt Pauline's and Jeremiah Godfrey's deaths from Uncle Henry's desk drawer and handed a few of them, along with her notes from their conversation with Louis, to

Rick. "Spread these pages across that side of the desk. I'll lay Pauline's pages here next to them."

Rick set the first page on the desk's upper left corner. "It's a timeline. Is there one for Pauline too?"

"Right here." Alex placed Pauline's timeline next to Jeremiah's and scanned both pages. Jeremiah's contained only a few more facts than those she and Rick had learned from Louis. One was citizens had reported that Jeremiah had appeared overexerted during the ball game but looked better after the picnic. Another was the police had found Jeremiah dead the next morning. And still another was a list of clues they'd found around his body: he'd been wearing bed clothes, an empty teacup sat on the end table next to his bed, his mouth was frozen in an open grimace, and he had swollen, dark blue lips and blue fingers. The details were all rather methodic and unemotional.

When Alex read Pauline's timeline, though, a lump filled her throat. The morning of December 1, 1873, at breakfast, had had been the last time Alex had seen her aunt. At 11:00 a.m., an unexpected visitor arrived—Theodore Clemens. He was one of Aunt Pauline's old beau. His lunch visit with Pauline triggered a heated argument between her and Uncle Henry, during which Theodore was asked to leave.

Soon after that, Aunt Pauline's health deteriorated. She complained of feeling sick, and she became increasingly irritable with the household staff. She also had a brief, tense interaction with Fay, where Aunt Pauline harshly told her to "Get out." By evening, Aunt Pauline was bedridden in a guest room.

Then, at 7:00 a.m. on December 2, Uncle Henry discovered her dead in the guest room. She wore her night robe, her bedding was pulled up over her waist, her dinner tray lay untouched on the end table next to the door, and a dead plant sat on top of the bureau.

Ivy jumped to the floor.

"You're either getting better," Alex said to her, "or you're feeling braver."

Ivy stood on her hind legs against the chair but didn't jump into Alex's lap. *Progress*. And definitely a good thing. Yet Alex's arms ached with an unexpected emptiness.

"One similarity I see between the timelines," Rick said, "is Jeremiah and Pauline had breakfast with their families the day they died. Pauline's timeline mentions you were there. Do you remember anything more than what your uncle wrote about that day?"

"Only that I was most put out for near an hour. Aunt Pauline had declared my penmanship a perfect disgrace, and if not immediately corrected, could doom me to spinsterhood."

Rick, smiling, crossed his arms and leaned back in his chair. "I never considered penmanship an important trait in a suitable wife."

Alex shrugged and focused on Ivy. Only Ivy.

"You won't ask me what I do think is important, will you?" Rick said.

"Why should I?"

Ivy crept toward the fireplace. Halfway there, her fur lit up like one of Mr. Thomas Edison's incandescent lamps. What had caused that?

"Confidence," Rick continued. "Determination, intelligence . . . and it doesn't hurt that you're beautiful. Alex? Are you listening to me?"

Alex, still facing Ivy, waved off his comment as if it wasn't important. As if she hadn't heard the exasperation—the disappointment?—in his voice.

Rick scooted his chair closer to hers. "Have you figured out why Ivy lights up like that?"

She shook her head. "I wish I'd at least found a way to trigger it. It could have helped me through a lot of dark spaces."

"I thought I was giving you a pet, not a lamp." A soft, dry chuckle.

Alex, pretending she didn't hear him, turned back to the files. She flipped through what appeared to be Pauline's small housekeeping account book and set it on the desk below the fact sheets.

Rick's knee bumped hers. "Alex? Are you listening to me?"

Too much, actually. Alex bit the inside of her cheeks. Time to get their conversation back to business. "All I remember is Pauline seemed out of sorts that day."

"But Jeremiah was his usual self—according to Louis."

"Maybe Louis didn't notice anything different because Jeremiah was always cross with him."

"Maybe."

Alex scanned between the timelines. "But they did both feel ill at some point that day."

Rick pushed up from his chair and walked to the window. "Not for the same length of time, though, or even after similar events. Your aunt spent the day with an old beau, and Jeremiah spent the day at work and at the ballpark."

Alex set the remaining papers from Pauline's file next to her timeline.

Rick returned to Alex's side and rested his hand on her shoulder.

An airy giggle trickled over the air.

Alex coughed. "That wasn't me."

"It sounded like you," Rick said.

She studied the red curtains for any hidden shapes. She'd once hid behind them when Aunt Pauline had been upset with her for adding two humps to her cursive *m* rather than three.

"I know the voice is like mine, but it wasn't. Do you see me smiling? Even a little bit? I can't imagine I'd laugh without smiling."

Rick's eyes lit up. "No, but you are radiant."

"Please be serious."

Another gentle, ghostly laugh—a masculine one this time. Rick's? But when she looked up at him, he shook his head.

The hair on the back of Alex's neck stiffened to attention. She stood and carefully peered about the room. "Is someone there?"

Ivy, her fur glowing like white fire, leapt into Alex's arms. Rick grasped her elbow. His fingers felt warm and firm against her skin. "There's no place in here for anyone to hide. Confess. You laughed just now, didn't you?"

She pulled away from him. "No, I did not."

"Don't think I mind. I love it, actually. I haven't heard you laugh so freely in over a year."

"I did not laugh, and I'm quite certain you didn't laugh a moment ago, either."

"You have me there, but give me a minute. I'm sure I can come up with something that'll make us both laugh." He, tapping his forefinger against his pursed lips, paced toward the fireplace. "I know. Who is the greatest chicken killer in Shakespeare?"

"This isn't a joke." Alex, scanning back and forth across the room, backed against the chalkboard. That way, if someone was hiding in the office, he or she couldn't grab her from behind.

"Macbeth," Rick said, "because he did murder most foul."

Alex groaned.

Rick peeked behind the settee and returned to her side. "Perhaps there's a legendary being in the room who doesn't want us to find out the truth about your aunt's or Mr. Godfrey's deaths. The Night Hag, maybe."

"Don't be ridiculous. The Night Hag is merely a mythological explanation for what must be a natural or perhaps a luminal phenomenon." Alex closed her eyes and shuffled through her memories like they were a stack of unconnected puzzle pieces: Ivy lighting up now and in the dark cavern, the voice that had whispered from somewhere within the cave, the laughs she and Rick had just heard. What could have caused them?

She took a deep breath, held it, and focused her mystiobiological senses on the furniture, the walls and ceiling, the fireplace, and even the fixtures, but nothing stirred within her luminal senses. "The sounds didn't come from anything inanimate."

"I figured you'd say that," Rick said. "What then? A luminal entity?"

"I don't know. I can't explain it."

"There are a lot of things out there I can't explain, either."

"*Rick.*"

Rick stared at Alex. She gaped, and despite herself, her fingers trembled against Ivy's fur. That was her voice, but—

"Your lips didn't move," he said.

She shook her head.

He narrowed his gaze and stepped away from the desk. "Who's in here?" he called into the room.

Alex pressed her body tighter against the blackboard, but this time it wasn't because she worried someone might grab her from behind. This time, she knew when and where she'd said Rick's name in just that way. It was the day she and Rick had ducked into this office for a few moments of privacy after the picnic where Uncle Henry and Rick's parents had announced her and Rick's engagement. She and Rick, laughing at their elders' naiveté, had stood close to the fireplace. Yes, Rick was wealthy, and Alex was well connected. And yes, they enjoyed each other's company, but their parents' insistence that she and Rick would eventually learn to love, not just like, each other was an illusion. Both she and Rick knew their own minds and would always know them. Partners, of course. Lovers, too, since all would expect an heir. But twisted, messy, romantic feelings for one another? Ridiculous!

Rick caught his breath.

Alex clenched her fists. Had he heard—remembered—that moment too? If he had, what then?

"Read aloud what your papers say," Alex said, "then I'll read mine. If we ignore the voices, maybe they'll go away."

"Ignore them? Not investigate? That doesn't sound like you."

She swallowed. Some memories had to stay in the past. "What would be the point? As you said, there's no one here."

"This might be your chance to meet a new luminal creature. And ethereal one."

"I'd rather not right now. Perhaps another day."

"All right. It's your call." He scanned the room yet again then slid a list of notes in front of them on the desk. "This one says, 'The Night Hag is a legendary demon who comes upon her victims just before they fall asleep or just before they wake. She paralyzes them and sits on their chests until they suffocate to death. Those who've survived the phenomenon report feelings of panic, drowning, or pain, and they claim they saw a witch in their room."

"Come here, Alex." Once more, the voice—Rick's voice—came from the direction of the fireplace.

Alex hugged Ivy tighter. *Ignore it.* But the memory came anyway. After Rick had said those words, he'd pulled her into his arms, kissed her softly on the lips, and with their noses touching said, "I know this feels strange between us now, but it won't always. I promise."

Alex shoved her thoughts back to the present and stared at Ivy. She'd stopped glowing.

Rick noticed too. He touched his forefinger to his lips, indicating she remain quiet, and the two listened. They stood there, not moving, barely breathing for several long moments. At length, Rick said, "I think the voices have stopped."

Alex furrowed her brows. "Do you suppose those two things are connected? Ivy's curious luminescence and those peculiar sounds?"

"I don't know. If not, they're highly coincidental."

"I place little faith in coincidence."

"Neither do I. Let's keep watch on that."

Rick turned over the paper he was examining—there was nothing on the back—and flipped again to the front. His hands trembled slightly. "At the top, your uncle wrote: 'Theodore Clemens already dead. He's not the killer.'"

Alex shuffled through a few more sheets of notes about her aunt. "I can see why Uncle Henry thought Mr. Clemens was responsible for her death. Listen to this. 'Theodore Clemens has a history of thievery. When the police questioned him, they found a skeleton key that would fit in our front door lock. We, however, found nothing missing, and Clemens did not possess any of our belongings. He claimed he had planned to rob us but hadn't yet done so, and since the police found nothing to connect Mr. Clemens to Pauline's death, and since a man cannot be convicted of a crime he didn't commit, they did not arrest him for theft, either.'"

Ivy jumped from Alex's arms, sat, and licked her shoulder. Alex surveyed the now silent space around the fireplace. Had whatever it was that had been in the room left?

"Go ahead," Rick said. "Read the rest of it."

"'Police questioned Pauline's family, servants, and Mrs. York,'" Alex read, "'but they learned nothing of consequence. Full reports are kept at the police station.' This is interesting. Uncle Henry included a complete description of the guest room and its contents at the time of Aunt Pauline's death. I wonder why he wrote all this when he could have just looked at the real thing. He hasn't allowed anyone to touch that room for any purpose other than an occasional light cleaning. Is there a list like this in Mr. Godfrey's file?"

"No. Let's make one after our visit there tomorrow."

Alex returned the paper to the desk and strode to the door that led into the formal dining room. Rick, stepping in beside her, clasped her hand and slowly wrapped her fingers around his bent elbow. "Whatever happened just now brought back a lot of old feelings."

Alex swallowed. She stared at a dent in the wood floor. If only her hands weren't sweating.

"Only those feelings aren't so old to me anymore," he added. "They're current."

"Please don't say such things."

"Why not? We're married."

"Somewhat."

He stepped in front of her, facing her, and placed his fingertips beneath her chin. He lifted her gaze to his. "We should be together, Alex."

Not again. Alex folded her arms in front of her. "Let's just try to get through this investigation, all right?"

"And then what?"

A shiver trembled through her as dishes from the dining room clanged like soft, accusing death tolls. "Then we'll see."

Chapter 8

THE GODFREY'S WHITE TIMBER home on the edge of town resembled the saltbox structured dollhouse Alex and Fay had shared. The house even had a steep roof, spanning from the two-story front to the single-story back. There were two differences, though: a white picket fence surrounded a yard of long brown grass, and tan curtains covered every window. Had someone closed them after Mr. Godfrey had died? Or had Mr. Godfrey kept them like that? Maybe because he'd been gone so much of the time?

"This way," Captain Sutter, Uncle Henry's policeman friend, said. He had hair as thin and white as Uncle Henry's, and the narrowness of his physique was also similar, but the pinkness of his cheeks was such a healthy contrast to her uncle's pallor that she had to blink five times to stop tears from clouding her eyes. *Don't miss him yet. He's still alive.*

"Mrs. Dalton?" Captain Sutter adjusted the black belt around the middle of his dark blue, button-up uniform jacket.

"Oh—I'm sorry. Yes." She shifted Ivy between her arms and straightened the sleeves of her white Georgiana blouse. She stepped through the gate Captain Sutter held open for her.

"Are you well?" Rick, behind her, dabbed his white handkerchief to the perspiration on his forehead.

"Well enough. Let's just finish this."

Rick inhaled sharply, but ignoring him, Alex strode over the grass growing through the cracks in the stone path to the front door. She stepped over the threshold into the narrow entry hall, which was lit only by the sunlight shining through the open doorway. She shivered.

"You can't possibly be cold." Rick unbuttoned the coat of his matching suit. "I don't remember July mornings here ever being this hot."

She checked her blue touring hat, making sure it still lay securely on her head, and crossed her arms tighter around Ivy. *Why'd Rick choose that matching suit today?* It was a darker blue than her twill bustle skirt, but everyone—Edna, Uncle Henry's other servants, even Captain Sutter—had given them appraising glances. Edna had even asked if they'd intentionally coordinated their clothing.

"I don't know why I shivered," Alex replied. "It's probably nothing."

"I doubt that."

Alex arched an eyebrow. After all she and Rick had been through and all she'd said to him, he still trusted her shivers? The other members of the Luminal Science Society hadn't even accepted her sensitivities until she'd found a luminal žaltys snake, but Rick had believed her the moment she'd mentioned them.

Captain Sutter motioned to the parlor on their right. Someone had torn out a six inch rectangle of the Courier and Ives wall paper. A patch of rough plaster filled the space between a large pale green leaf and a faded yellow flower.

"Where would you like to begin?" Captain Sutter said.

Ivy jabbed her claws through Alex's blouse.

"Mercy! What provoked that, kitty?" Alex pulled her cat away from her shoulder.

"Maybe she needs a break from that position," Rick said. "Let me carry her." But when he reached for Ivy, Ivy hissed at him and clung sharper to Alex.

Rick yanked back his hand. "Maybe we should have left her at the manor."

"And let her out of my sight? Not until I'm certain she's well, and I figure out what causes her to—" She nodded to Captain Sutter. "—behave as she does."

Rick's eyes glinted, but he didn't smile.

Alex drew back her shoulders. "Let's inspect Mr. Godfrey's bedroom first," she said to Captain Sutter. *Since Aunt Pauline also died in her bedchamber.*

"As you wish." Captain Sutter opened the flaking white-painted door at the end of the hall and stepped inside a narrow, enclosed stairway. The steps led like a tunnel to the top floor.

Rick touched Alex's elbow. "Is that the reason you kept Mary's clothes?" His whisper sounded more like a sigh of realization than a question. Had he really not understood why she'd gathered everything that had been with Mary when the sheriff had found her body?

"Of course."

Rick swallowed. "I thought you kept them to—" He shook his head.

"To what?"

"Never mind."

She didn't ask him about it again, but the sudden tightness in his lips and the paleness of his skin indicated what he wouldn't say. Either he believed she hadn't been able to part with what remained of their daughter, which was true, or he'd thought she'd saved them as a reminder meant to punish him. Yet, if he thought her capable of such cruelty, why would he still wish to be with her?

Because he loves me.

Alex blinked that thought away, turned away from Rick, and stepped up the creaky wooden stairs to the second floor.

On the landing, a small table covered with a dusty white tablecloth stood against the wall directly in front of them. Splinters flaked from its legs as if someone had chipped at it with a small knife. The open, empty wardrobe beside the table bore similar damage, its wooden surfaces showing identical marks. Two additional doors flanked the remaining walls.

Captain Sutter smoothed his mustache and opened the door at their left. "Mr. Godfrey's room is here. We've taken the bedding to the station for further scrutiny, but everything else is as it was when we found his body."

Alex curled her toes. If only she could have examined the scene before the police had altered the evidence. True, Captain Sutter had graciously supplied her with a list of what the police had found, but experience had taught her they often overlooked critical, and especially luminal, points.

Rick caught her eye. "Too bad my wife wasn't here then," he said to the captain. "She'd have likely doubled your list."

"I assure you, my men are among the best detectives in the state."

Alex peered between the two men, but when her gaze locked on Rick's, her cheeks warmed. That intense look again. *My knees will not buckle!*

"We have more to worry about than who is capable of doing what," she said, "and I, for one, would like to get on with the investigation."

"Of course." Captain Sutter opened the closest door and motioned her and Rick inside the room.

Mr. Godfrey's spacious chamber had an A-frame wall, a black walnut floor, and stained pale yellow wallpaper. The furniture—feather bed, storage chest, bureau, and rocking chair—were badly neglected or damaged like the rest of the house she'd so far seen. Even the plain tan curtains were torn and frayed. Did men truly care so little about what they saw every day once the women in their lives were gone?

She glanced at Rick. He still stood in the doorway, watching her with those stormy sea-hazel eyes that made her fingers ache and her mouth water as if she'd just eaten a newly-picked golden apple. She turned away from him. And swallowed. That assumption—what she'd just wondered about men—was wrong. The men she knew on a personal basis, men like Rick did care—or at least notice—the things *and people* around them.

Alex stepped into the room and took a deep breath. "Nothing so far." *Nothing luminal, that is.*

Captain Sutter lifted a gray eyebrow over his even grayer eyes. "Are you looking for something in particular?"

Rick strolled toward the bed, and Alex set Ivy on the floor. The cat stayed close to her feet.

"I won't know what I'm looking for until I sense it," she said.

She again scanned the room, but the only thing similar to Aunt Pauline's bedchamber was the rocking chair. If the Night Hag had indeed killed Mr. Godfrey, wouldn't the chair be closer to the bed, like the chair that had been in Aunt Pauline's room? Local lore indicated that those who'd survived a Night Hag attack had first seen the demon sitting in a rocking chair close to the bed. But then, did folklore believe the demon brought her own rocking chair with her?

"Has any of the furniture been moved?" she added.

Captain Sutter pressed his lips into a tight line. "Everything here is as it was when we arrived."

"Oh, yes. You said that." Alex moved closer to the bed and sniffed. A hint of spice. Was it ginger? "Did anyone find food containers in here?"

"I don't believe so."

Rick sidled closer to her. "What is it?"

Alex pretended she didn't notice the feel of his arm pressed against hers and sniffed again. "What about a wine glass?"

"No glass," Captain Sutter said. "We did find wine spilled on Mr. Godfrey's nightshirt, though, along with some of his dinner."

"Uncle Henry's notes said Jeremiah hadn't felt well."

"That is correct."

Rick stepped away from Alex and crossed to the back wall. He pushed aside the curtain. Hazy light flashed over his hair the way it had the first day she'd seen him standing in the Watson's front doorway, and for a moment she couldn't breathe. Why did good memories so often prompt heartache?

"Did Mr. Godfrey and the boy live alone?" Rick asked the captain. "This window doesn't look like it's been cleaned in ages. The sill's covered with spider webs."

"They did live alone."

Alex paced between the bed and bureau. Something niggled at her thoughts. What was it? She tapped her lip, sifting through the sparse facts: sickness, wine, a possible cry of pain. "Is it certain Mr. Godfrey wasn't poisoned?"

Captain Sutter's stare narrowed so tightly she couldn't tell if it was with admiration or surprise. "We did take that possibility into consideration, Mrs. Dalton, but the only poison we found was arsenic in rattraps in the kitchen and cellar. The medical examiner didn't find any poison in Mr. Godfrey's body, either."

"No poison he knew about, you mean."

"I assure you the man's quite thorough."

Rick stepped between Alex and Captain Sutter. "I'm sure the examiner was thorough, as far as the modern sciences are concerned, but Mrs. Dalton is quite well versed in, shall we say, unconventional substances."

Captain Sutter rolled his eyes. "Your interest in the luminal, you mean?"

"I *am* a mystiobiologist." Why hadn't Uncle Henry informed her his policeman friend was a skeptic? Alex folded her arms, gave him a hard smile, and added, "What's more, there's a scent in this room that reminds me of a highly toxic flower found only in mountainous meadows."

"It kills some and heals others, I suspect. Many so-called luminal products make similar claims."

"It is not hype, Sir. It's science. And Monk's Bane only kills."

"Nevertheless, if it is a real substance, I'm sure our examiner would have found it."

A *real* substance? It was a good thing Alex hadn't brought Alistair with her. She had a good mind to set him on top of the captain's head just to see if he'd recognize Alistair was *real*.

"I don't wish to offend you," Captain Sutter continued. "Your uncle speaks highly of your deductive skills, and I trust his judgment. But I have also seen and arrested enough luminal snake oil salesmen to know their claims are rarely true. And when I say rarely, I am being generous."

Alex opened her mouth. How dare he be so—so rudely narrow-minded? But before she could confront him about his prejudice, Rick clasped her elbow. "Shall we move on?"

Rick's voice sent a warm, unwelcome shiver through her, and she scowled. *I don't want to feel comfort now.*

"Yes, of course. This way." Captain Sutter led them from Mr. Godfrey's room to Louis's bedroom across the hall.

The boy's bedchamber contained even fewer furnishings than Mr. Godfrey's did and was in need of much greater repair. The blankets heaped at the foot of the small trundle bed were torn in several places, and the wardrobe had more nicks and scrapes than any of the finish work she'd so far seen. A large wooden crate sat against the wall beneath the window, and a pencil lay beside it on the floor. His writing desk?

Rick stepped next to her again. The floor creaked beneath his weight. "Notice anything?"

"The scent's not in here, but—" She walked to the window and pulled back the tan curtain. While there weren't any spider webs on these ledges, a single dead plant was draped over the edge of a cracked brown flowerpot.

"Monk's Bane?" Rick asked.

"No. Monk's Bane has purple flowers." She leaned over the wilted salmon-colored flower and took a deep breath. Nothing stirred or tingled within her. It was possible that might be because the plant had lost its life force, but more likely, "It's a simple geranium."

She looked over her shoulder at Captain Sutter. She expected to see an emotionless stare, but instead he looked down at his boots. Ivy had planted herself on top of them.

"Come here, kitty," Alex said.

Ivy slowly stood, as if she were the only being in the world with anywhere to go, and walked to Alex. Alex crouched down to her, and Ivy leapt into her arms.

"You don't think it's the Night Hag, do you?" Rick said.

Alex hugged her cat. "I never did, but now I'm even more of that opinion. Let's move on."

Captain Sutter nodded, straightened his uniform jacket, and headed for the door. His footsteps clomped smartly across the wood floor.

"What makes you certain it's not the Night Hag?" Rick added. "Because of the Monk's Bane?"

"In part. But really, Rick. Demons? It sounds like an exaggerated fairytale."

"You're forgetting I've seen and fought several, as you call them, fairytales." Rick motioned for her to walk with him from the room.

"Very well. I'll concede there are disembodied forces in this world, but I don't believe they can kill. You're still alive, aren't you?"

"I was the last time I checked." He caught hold of her hand, stopping her at the top of the staircase.

Warmth, strength, skin.

"Do you agree?" he pressed. "Am I alive?"

Alex lowered her gaze and retrieved her hand before the foolish thing perspired even more. "Be serious, Rick."

"I am serious." His breath wisped across her forehead.

"Mr. and Mrs. Dalton?" Captain Sutter called from the bottom of the stairs.

Rick straightened. He took a deep breath. "Coming," he replied. He again held his hand out to Alex. "Shall we?"

She folded her arms and started down the stairs ahead of him. "However," she continued as if nothing had interrupted their conversation, "while we've both seen things we can't fully explain, I have never seen abilities with the power to act for themselves. Have you?"

He trailed close behind her. "No."

"It follows, then, that abilities, powers, energies—whatever you want to call them—are controlled by a physical entity, and since disembodied forces don't have physical bodies, one couldn't have killed Mr. Godfrey. The murderer has to be a person."

"Disembodied forces aren't *abilities*, But I will agree with you on this point. While many people, including mystiobiologists, have dealt with them, I have never heard of one killing a human being. Only controlled them. Or influenced them to destroy themselves."

"Neither Mr. Godfrey nor my aunt destroyed themselves."

"Of course. Poison, then?"

"Monk's Bane, yes. That's my strongest theory."

"So we're looking for a plant with a purple flower."

"Yes. Or anything that smells odd but not unpleasant."

Chapter 9

A LEX DIDN'T EVEN HAVE to enter the parlor, which was similar in size and structure to Mr. Godfrey's bedroom, to sense there was nothing luminal inside. Still, she perused it anyway so no one could question her findings later. Two wood chairs with spool-turned legs—one of them broken—a faded red circular sofa, and a small lack-luster end table. A plain gray rock fireplace filled the far right corner of the outside walls.

"Why don't you let me carry Ivy for a while?" Rick said. "I'm sure your arms could use a break."

Alex petted Ivy's head. "You're brave to want to try that again."

"Nonsense! I've faced much more frightening foes than her. Several times, in fact."

"None with claws."

"I'll take my chances."

"Very well. But if she scratches you, don't set her down. I don't know where that rat poison is."

"Or the Monk's Bane."

"Exactly." Alex handed Ivy to Rick, but the moment she released her, Ivy stiffened her spine and stared at Alex as if she'd betrayed her.

"Be good." Alex watched to see if Ivy would disobey her and scratch Rick, but she didn't. In truth, Ivy had never scratched Rick, despite her obvious dislike of him.

Captain Sutter led them on through the dining room. As they passed the mahogany dining table, Alex ran her gloved finger across the top and then sniffed the powdery dust. The same gingery-sweet scent she'd smelled in Mr. Godfrey's bedchamber wafted over her.

"Monk's Bane?" Rick said.

"I believe so." Again, she sniffed her fingers. "It certainly smells like Monk's Bane, but I don't sense Monk's Bane's life force."

"Something else then?"

"Maybe."

They continued on to the kitchen. Shelves of dishes covered the wall across from them, and there was another door to their right. However, Alex's attention latched onto the mounds of dead black ants lying on top of the food-preparation table directly in front of them.

Captain Sutter cleared his throat. "Forgive me, Mrs. Dalton. I can assure you nothing of this sort was here when my colleagues and I went through the house earlier. Come. We can leave."

"Don't concern yourself, sir. I'm not offended in the least." Alex stepped closer to the ants. She scanned from the piles of their bodies and down to the clean floor. *Shouldn't there be ants down there too?*

"Look here, Alex." Rick, still holding Ivy against his chest, crouched in the corner next to the other door. He motioned to the floor beneath the lowest shelf. "This must be one of those traps Captain Sutter spoke of."

She followed his gaze to the corner beneath the cupboard. A partially-eaten round ball of what appeared to be hardened cornmeal lay a few inches away from the wall, and a dead rat lay a few feet from it. It didn't stink of death, though, so the body had likely been there for some time.

She looked up at Captain Sutter. "Do you have gloves with you, sir?"

"I do." Captain Sutter pulled a set of slender black gloves from his suit coat pockets, put them on, and lowered onto his hands and knees. After he retrieved the ball, he held it out to Alex and Rick.

Alex took the solid lump. She sniffed it. "Cornmeal, to be sure, and some type of hardening agent."

"I'd bet my hat it also contains arsenic," Captain Sutter said. "We found, removed, and tested a container of this stuff on the shelf there, along with several dough balls like this one. They all contained arsenic."

"I expect you're right. Like this ball, arsenic is odorless and has no luminal properties." She turned her attention back to the ants. "This, on the other hand, is quite extraordinary."

Rick followed her back to the table. "A luminal substance?"

"I'm not sure yet." She lowered her face closer to the tabletop. "Every couple of breaths or so, I get a tiny whiff of something. I don't know what it is, but look here. What could have caused these insects to behave so unnaturally? Hundreds of ants swarmed to this exact spot and died. We can deduce something lured them there, but since I can see no other ants, dead or alive, in this room, I must assume they all went there and died immediately."

"Unlike that rat over there," Rick said. "It moved half a dozen feet before it succumbed to its fate."

"Exactly. Poisons, especially luminal ones, generally affect all creatures in the same way."

"So it's something other than luminal."

"I didn't say that."

Rick handed Ivy back to Alex, looked under the table, and knocked on its side. "Perhaps there really wasn't anything on it when the police went through the house, because the table itself is poisonous. Or, more likely, cursed like the treasure my partners are currently hunting for. I know this may sound outrageous, but stay with me on this. What if this table is cursed and Mr. Godfrey unwittingly discovered it in a basement or an attic or someplace? And what if he only recently brought it into this house? What if the table killed him?"

Alex held back a smile. Rick possessed a keen intellect, yet his imagination oft ran away from him. It was best to go along with him for a time before reeling him back to reality. "Louis didn't say anything about Jeremiah having brought a new table into the house."

"We didn't ask him, either. Think about it, Alex. There is nothing on this table, and yet those ants died on top of it. It has to be the table. It—I know! It housed the soul of an evil demon who finally found a way out." His eyes widened. "That's it! This table belonged to the Night Hag."

"That's your conclusion? I thought we agreed that a person, not a demon, killed Jeremiah Godfrey and Aunt Pauline."

"We could have been wrong about that."

Alex pursed her lips. While she had joined Rick on a few of his treasure-hunting expeditions, she hadn't gone with him and his partners to New Zealand where they'd hunted for Thunderroot, discovered Ivy, and found the White Lions of God's Lost Thunder Drum. Most people considered his adventures as outlandish tales, but when Rick had described them to her, both his voice and his expressions had burned through her with the sound of truth. She'd believed him just as much as he'd believed her about her luminal sensitivities. Didn't he then deserve the benefit of a doubt?

"Perhaps we were wrong," she agreed.

Captain Sutter tilted his head. "You two aren't serious?"

"Can you think of a better explanation?" Rick asked.

The captain gaped at him, but said nothing more.

"What's through that other door?" Alex said.

"The cellar."

"May we?"

"Certainly." Captain Sutter took an oil lamp from the shelf next to the cellar door, lit it, and headed down the staircase. At the bottom, he hunched beneath the low ceiling. Rick did too, but Alex, cradling Ivy, stood upright. Ivy's claws dug through her blouse. Ivy might be feeling better, but she was still afraid of the dark.

Captain Sutter moved to the center of the shadowy, square room. Dust particles floated through the air around the lamp's flame, spider webs straddled the corners of the room, and dead bug bodies spotted the floor.

Alex sneezed. "I don't think this place has been used in a while."

"I believe you're right, Mrs. Dalton."

Rick handed her a clean handkerchief.

"Thank you." She pressed it over her mouth and nose. *Much better.*

"Is there anything luminal in here?" Rick said close to her ear.

"I'm afraid to sniff. If that dust irritates my allergies, I'll be awake all night."

"I'll stay up with you, if you'd like."

She smiled beneath the handkerchief. "That's nice of you, but I'll manage." She stepped out of the dust particles and walked to the stone wall at her right. She then removed the handkerchief and breathed inward. No tingles. "So far the room feels even deader of luminal life than the rest of the house."

Ivy's fur lit up like a ball of lightning.

Alex lifted her upright in front of her. She stared hard into her face. "What causes you to do that?"

"What is it?" Captain Sutter whispered. He backed away from Alex and Rick. "Witchcraft!"

"Not in the least," Alex said. "Ivy is simply a luminal animal."

"She has the astonishing ability to glow," Rick clarified. "But Mrs. Dalton hasn't yet figured out how or why she even does it."

Ivy squirmed out of Alex's hands, jumped to the floor, and raced to the basement's back wall. She crouched in front of it with her muscles tensed and her fur, still glowing, standing on end.

"Come back here, Ivy!" Alex said.

A child whimpered behind her.

Alex, Rick, and Captain Sutter whirled to the sound.

"What was that?" Captain Sutter said.

"No. Please!" the voice cried.

The hair on the back of Alex's neck stood straight up. She scanned the walls, the ceiling, the floor. That was Louis's voice, but Louis wasn't there. Where was it coming from?

"Stop your whining!" a deep male voice said. "You'll stay down there 'til you've learned to obey your master."

Alex inched closer to the sound. She scanned the wall, the floor, the ceiling, but saw nothing but stone and dirt.

"I'll obey. I promise! Please don't shut me up here in the dark!"

Alex's stomach turned over. Were the voices coming from the walls? It seemed ridiculous, yet where else could they be coming from?

A sharp, crisp crack echoed through the room. Scuffing sounds then skidded down the stairs. A door slammed. Louis's wails became soft sobs.

Dear God in heaven, please don't let this be real. Alex prayed the words inside her mind, not as a plea for help but to comfort her heart, because everything inside her knew the sounds were real. Just as real as those she and Rick had heard in her uncle's office. *Back when Ivy had glowed!*

Alex blinked. Were the ghostly voices in some way connected to Ivy's luminal power?

Rick grabbed Alex's arm. "Let's get out of here."

Ivy charged up the stairs ahead of them. Alex, Rick, and Captain Sutter raced after her. They didn't stop until the four of them stood near the outside front gate. Ivy, no longer glowing, jumped into Alex's arms, and Alex, suddenly overpowered by pent-up emotions, moved into Rick's open arms. She pressed her head against his chest. Had Mary known the terror Alex had heard in Louis's voice?

Rick held Alex tighter. She clung to his waist. His strength and comfort flowed over her like morning sunlight.

Several minutes passed.

Finally, she pulled herself together, wiped her eyes, and stepped away from him.

The three stared at one another.

"What was that?" Captain Sutter said.

The paleness in both men's faces and the brightness in their eyes told Alex they, like she, knew exactly what they'd heard.

"Jeremiah Godfrey was a monster," Rick said at last.

"No wonder Louis prayed the Night Hag would kill him," Captain Sutter said.

"What?" Alex said.

Captain Sutter frowned. "I'm not surprised he didn't tell you. He said it once—only once—when my colleagues and I first questioned him after we found Mr. Godfrey's body. But from what we heard—if anyone did that to my son, I'd kill him."

"No one would blame you," Rick said.

Alex swallowed. Louis had been the only one in the house when Jeremiah had died—*opportunity*. The scent of Monk's Bane in the house along with Jeremiah's earlier illness indicated poisoning—*means*. Wanting to escape abuse, praying for Jeremiah's death—*motive*. "Except the law," Alex said. "The law would blame anyone for killing Jeremiah Godfrey, even under those circumstances."

Both men stared hard at each other and turned to Alex.

"We don't know anything," Rick said.

"More important, we can't prove anything," Captain Sutter said. "The coroner listed Jeremiah Godfrey's cause of death as unexplained, and as far as I'm concerned, that description still stands."

Alex faced the road. They had no tangible proof of who'd killed Jeremiah Godfrey, but she knew, and Rick and Captain Sutter indicated they knew, that the facts pointed to Louis. Would it be right to force a young boy—a child who'd faced such abuse—to face the penal system for murder?

"I do think we should tell Uncle Henry what we've learned, though," she said.

Chapter 10

ALMOST AS SOON AS Alex and Rick stepped inside Watson Manor, a servant standing as stiff and straight as his pressed suit handed Rick a telegram.

Rick glanced at Alex, read the note, and frowned. "I need you to send a reply," he said to the servant.

"Yes, Sir."

Alex knew that expression. Rick's telegram had to be news from one of his partners about the treasure they were hunting. That meant Rick would be leaving soon.

Of course.

She set her jaw, turned away from Rick, and headed to the stairway.

"Alex, wait," Rick said.

"I'll meet you in Uncle Henry's bedchamber," she called over her shoulder.

But she didn't go straight to Uncle Henry's room. She stopped at hers and carefully folded, refolded, and finally laid a blanket in the corner rocking chair. "Take a nice nap," she crooned to Ivy as she set her on top of it. "The windows are locked, and I'll close the door behind me when I leave. No one will bother you."

Ivy sighed and relaxed into the blanket's softness.

Alex sighed too and placed her hat on top of the bureau, but neither action settled her. She folded her arms. She paced between the wardrobe, where Alistair stood in his jar, and the bed. Some-one—perhaps the maid—had tucked the blankets so tightly that the mattress was smooth as a game board. They'd laughed, bargained, and competed for each other's favorite pieces, with Rick ultimately winning. Triumphant, he'd then left with his business partners to explore a nearby canyon, drawn by rumors of a bank robber's hidden loot.

She'd laughed about it at the time and called him a "little boy" when he hadn't returned until the next morning—because she and Rick were friends, and friends let friends live their own lives. But friends also didn't leave when tough times came, like after Mary's death. And now Rick was about to leave her again, even though he now was more than just Alex's friend; he was Mary's father. And he'd said he'd help her find their daughter's killer.

Cold shivered through Alex. She ran her hands up and down her arms. Fortunately, she hadn't fully trusted his promise.

I will not be hurt this time. Please, God?

Alex stood taller, smoothed her loose hair strands back from her face, and stepped into the hall. She closed the door firmly behind her.

"I'm glad to see I didn't miss you." Rick leaned against the wall directly across the hall from her room. Had he waited for her?

Alex peered toward her uncle's bedchamber door at the end of the hall.

Rick looked at her empty arms and then back into her face. His eyes narrowed. "Where's Ivy? Everything all right?"

"It will be." Alex bustled past him and went to her uncle's door. She knocked.

Rick followed her.

"Come in," Uncle Henry called from inside.

Alex clasped the doorknob, but despite still telling herself that nothing was wrong, that it didn't matter that Rick would soon leave her to handle things alone *again*, her fingers trembled.

Rick wrapped his right hand around hers. The trembling stopped. "Don't worry about Louis," he said. "He'll be fine."

Alex bit her lower lip. Did Rick know how close he was to her? That if she edged a mere few inches to the right, she'd be within the crook of his arm? "That's easy enough for you to say, I suppose, since you won't have to worry about any of this for much longer."

"What makes you say that?"

She bit her tongue and shook her head. "Nothing." She turned the knob, but his grip tightened, stopping her.

"Tell me, Alex."

She lifted her gaze to his. Their bodies were so close she could feel his breath on her cheek. "The telegram the servant gave you when we arrived."

He didn't ask her what she meant, and she didn't offer an explanation, but at last he said, "You're wrong."

"It was from one of your partners, wasn't it?"

Rick didn't move—not his gaze, not his hand, not his body. Nor did he deny her accusation. "I didn't know I was so obvious."

"Come in, Alexandra," her uncle repeated from the other side of the door.

Alex moistened her lips. "Uncle Henry's waiting for us."

Rick's gaze wavered, but at last he released her hand, and she drew back her shoulders. *My arms do not ache. I do not miss Mary and—or anyone.*

They entered the room.

"The two of you look as if you've seen a ghost," Uncle Henry said.

"We almost did," Rick said.

Alex walked to her uncle's bedside. On the way back from the Godfrey's house, she'd silently rehearsed what she should say to him, but still the information felt uncomfortable on her lips. She, Rick, and Captain Sutter had chosen the right course, hadn't they?

"Just as you suspected," she began, "we found what might be luminal evidence that Mr. Godfrey was murdered. Poisoned, to be exact. But there is nothing in the deed that connects his death to Aunt Pauline's."

"Further scrutiny—"

"No, Uncle. In fact, circumstances are such that Captain Sutter, Rick, and I—all three of us—believe we should stop our investigation immediately and keep what we've learned to ourselves."

Uncle Henry's eyes widened. He glanced from one to the other of them. "Explain."

Alex tugged the lacy hem of her sleeve's cuff. At the same time, Rick stepped in behind her and briefly squeezed her shoulder. It was a simple touch, yet it was filled with his overpowering comfort. It gave her the strength she needed to recount the vile words they'd heard in the Godfrey's basement and their belief in Louis's guilt.

When she reached the end of it, she inhaled as if she'd dropped a great weight. "I'm sorry, Uncle. I know it's not the answer you'd wanted, but it does provide some closure."

Uncle Henry steepled his fingers. "It does not."

"Why so?"

When he didn't answer her, she pulled her gaze from his and paced to the window. "In any case, Rick and I have completed the task you gave us, and we respectfully request your blessing to leave Watson Manor after—" She pictured the tall, black wrought iron fence that divided the Watson's property from its neighbor. Its individual spires pointed to the heavens. To God.

"Say the rest of it, Alex," Uncle Henry said. "You want my blessing to leave *after I die.*"

Alex compressed her lips and turned back to him. She would not let emotion overpower her. Not there in front of those men.

"At any rate," Uncle Henry continued, "I'm not certain Rick agrees that you've completed your task and wish to leave Watson Manor."

Alex looked up at Rick. He gazed steadily back at her, his hazel eyes unblinking beneath his thick eyelashes, and instant heat rushed through her skin. She folded her arms in front of her. She glanced back to her uncle. It was a good thing she and Rick would soon part ways. She hadn't known it, but she apparently did have feelings for him. Specifically him. Not just friendly feelings, and not just because he was a man and she was a woman. Nor even because he was her wedded husband. She had feelings for *him.* And he would soon leave.

"This *is* a terrible business for Louis," Uncle Henry continued, "but if Sutter's fine with keeping the boy out of it, so am I. Besides that, Louis is too young to have killed Pauline, which means your investigation is not finished. True, the similarities between Mr. Godfrey's death and Pauline's may not prove that the same person killed them, but they do strengthen my conviction that my wife was murdered. I still need the two of you to find out who did it."

"You've always believed she was murdered, Uncle, and you had the evidence when it was fresh. There's nothing left for us to investigate."

"I don't believe that."

"You must. Rick and I have been through your files. We've examined Pauline's room. Maybe, if you had asked me to help you when the murder actually happened, I might have sensed something, because the evidence was fresh then. But now all luminal evidence, if there was any, dissipated years ago. It's over. Please let it rest."

Uncle Henry's facial muscles tightened. "Have you let Mary's death rest?"

"Mary's death is not like Pauline's. I don't have to prove my daughter was murdered. I only have to find the one who did it."

"And I still need to find the one who killed my wife."

"Maybe you already did," Rick said. "Maybe it was that Mr. Clemens, the man who died."

"Then prove it!" Uncle Henry said. "Prove it wasn't me!"

Alex did a double take. "You?" She and Rick spoke at the same time. "What do you mean?" Alex added.

Uncle Henry focused on something at the foot of his bed. Finally, he motioned to a black box on top of the fireplace mantle. "There's another file in there. Sutter copied it out for me. Apparently, I was once their strongest suspect. The police could never prove someone murdered Pauline, much less that I had committed the crime, but still some believed—still do believe—I killed her."

"That's ridiculous," Alex said.

"It certainly is." Rick retrieved the file from the box and handed it to Alex.

Alex opened it. She scanned the words and forced herself not to gape at the incriminating suppositions. How could anyone have written, much less believed, such terrible things about her uncle?

"Please clear my name before I die," Uncle Henry said.

"No one who knows you could possibly believe you had anything to do with Aunt Pauline's death." Alex squeezed the back of her neck. "And anyway, all that's in this file are unsubstantiated accusations."

He stared at her, and though he said nothing, images of Mary's and Aunt Pauline's faces filled the air between them. Both victims deserved justice. So did she and her uncle. And Rick.

"Why don't we think about this new development for a while?" Rick said to Alex. "I'm sure your uncle needs to rest."

"Yes," Uncle Henry said. "Leave me for now. But please don't wait too long to tell me you'll do it."

Alex sighed.

"Come, Alex," Rick said. "I daresay you need food. You didn't come down for breakfast this morning, and it's now nearly dinnertime."

"I haven't felt hungry."

"That may be, but your body needs sustenance." Rick moved ahead of her and opened the door.

"I'll be waiting for your answer," Uncle Henry added.

Alex frowned. There was no point in it, but how could she refuse him? "I'll do what I can, Uncle."

Rick turned back to her. At the same time, he pressed his free hand against his pocket where he'd put his telegram.

Alex's stomach knotted. Rick's movement was simple, small, and inconsequential. There was absolutely no reason it should bother her, no reason she should care that he would soon leave again. *I'm perfectly capable of taking care of myself and Uncle Henry's final request on my own.*

"Before you eat," Uncle Henry said, "would you please bring Pauline's file to me?"

"Yes," Alex said.

"Let me do it," Rick said. "I'm on my way out anyway, and you look like you'll faint if you don't get some food in you."

Alex turned away. Perhaps it was better to let him think food was her problem, to let him step out of her life while she still had family around her. It would make his final departure easier to accept. Wouldn't it?

"Very well," she said.

Chapter 11

"SIT YOURSELF DOWN," EDNA said when Alex stepped into the kitchen.

The late afternoon sunlight from the small basement window streamed behind Edna's graying brown hair in an almost-angelic halo. If only Louis had been blessed with someone as kind to him after his mother had died as Edna had been to Alex when she'd moved to Watson Manor.

"I was just preparing trays of food for you and Mr. Dalton to eat in your rooms," she added. "I hope I'm not overstepping my bounds, but seeing how pale you both were when you returned from the Godfrey's, I expected neither of you would feel up to coming down to dinner. And even if you did, it wouldn't hurt to get a little extra nourishment into you."

Alex sat at the worktable in the same chair she'd often sat in when she was girl. "Where's Cook?"

Edna ladled potato and clam chowder into a bowl she'd taken from atop one of two dinner trays. She set the bowl in front of Alex. "It's her day off. You wouldn't expect *her* to call a bowl of chowder an entire meal, would you?"

Alex smiled slightly and stared at her spoon. The steam from the chowder warmed her cheeks almost as deliciously as the clammy scent triggered its remembered taste. "No, I suppose not."

"You're upset," Edna said.

"I'm fine."

Edna sat in the chair across from her. "I've known you for a lot of years, my girl, and I recognize that look. You've gotten yourself into a mess that you don't know how to get out of, haven't you?"

Alex forced a laugh. "It's nothing that serious."

Edna's gaze narrowed.

Alex dipped her spoon inside the thick chowder and slowly stirred it, cooling it. "How's Louis doing?"

"Better than one might expect. He's a strong lad. That's all I can say."

Alex froze at the tightness in Edna's voice. She scrutinized the woman's protruding eyes, her clenched jaw, her flattened lips. Had she guessed at Louis's guilt? "What makes you say that?"

Red colored Edna's face. "I don't know what you mean."

"Yes, I believe you do."

Edna hastily rearranged the empty dishes on the tray Alex assumed she'd meant for Rick. "Children do not have the kinds of nightmares Louis has for no reason."

Alex touched Edna's arm. "I don't mean to upset you. I'm sorry. I only thought, as his caretaker, you might have recognized—something like that. But we'll keep it to ourselves, won't we?"

"Of course, my girl." Edna again rearranged the empty dishes then turned back to Alex. She looked her straight in the eyes. "But changing the subject from you to the boy isn't going to work. What is it? Are you missing your outdoor adventures? Your luminal work? Or—is it Mary?"

Alex lifted the creamy, steaming chowder to her lips and lowered it again. It was still too hot. "I wish I'd known what Uncle Henry wanted before I'd arrived."

"So it's Mr. Dalton."

The tears Alex had held back all day—no, since she'd first received the telegram—filled her eyes. She'd forgotten how easily Edna could read her expressions, forgotten how it felt to be so well known and loved, forgotten how quickly Edna could pull the truth from her heart. "How did you know?"

Edna's expression pinched. "When Mr. Dalton arrived the first time, the day before you did, and when he said you'd require separate bedrooms, it was easy enough to see something wasn't right."

"You didn't know about our separation until then?"

"Mr. Watson never spoke of it to me. Perhaps he didn't believe it was my place to know."

"I doubt that, Edna. He knows you love me. Mercy, he let you raise me."

"Perhaps he expected the two of you would mend things before there was any need to speak of it."

Alex brushed a large tear from the corner of her eye. "You might be right."

Edna handed Alex a dry dish towel, and Alex wiped her eyes.

"Rick and I shouldn't have married," Alex said after she'd regained some of her composure. "That's all there is to it. I don't know why I, or anyone, should be surprised things didn't work out between us."

"You have every right to be surprised, my girl. When two people marry, no matter the reason, they contract to love and care for each other as husband and wife for the rest of their lives."

Alex stirred the soup again, but though the mild aroma warmed through her, her stomach clenched. She slid the soup bowl away from her.

Edna watched the movement. "Did he hurt you?"

"Yes."

Edna stiffened. "He has a demon inside him. I did not know."

"That's not what I meant, Edna. Rick didn't hurt me physically. He's not a violent man. He—he did only what I told him to do." *He left.* Alex's lips trembled into a frown. "But it still hurts."

Edna placed her hand over Alex's. "Forgive an old woman for over-reacting. What did he do?"

"There's nothing to forgive. I should have thought before I spoke." Alex quickly recapped the events of what she'd said to Rick and what he'd said to her that day he'd left her. "Edna?"

"Yes?"

"Is it possible to get over the pain?"

The corners of Edna's eyes crinkled downward. "It might take a long time—years even. But eventually, when the hurt scabs over the pain will ease."

"Do you forget?"

Edna shrugged and looked away. "I haven't."

But you've learned to live with it. Alex didn't know where that thought came from, but when it came, she saw Edna with new eyes. Edna slipping her and Fay more cake than the cook believed was good for them. Edna standing between them and Aunt Pauline when their school assignments weren't completed as perfectly as they should be. Edna sleeping on the floor in their room when lightning storms frightened them. Alex had always believed Edna was like Athena, the Greek goddess of war, but now Alex saw her more as an immovable shield. She had been, and judging by the determined kindness that now shone from her gray eyes, she always would be Alex's and Fay's protector. No wonder Alex's aunt and uncle had put her in charge of the girls' upbringings. And yet, seeing her now through a woman's eyes, Alex realized Edna must have faced her own hardships.

"Did you ever marry?" Alex said.

"Yes. A long time ago."

"What happened?" Alex clamped her hand over her mouth. It wasn't polite to ask a woman why she wasn't married any longer. Heaven knew Alex hated such questions after Rick had left, and they, technically, were still married. Even so, how could Alex not have heard of Edna having been married? "I'm sorry. I misspoke."

"My husband died. And it's no great secret, so you needn't worry."

"Did you have children?"

Edna's eyes glazed. "They died as babies. A flu epidemic. It's also what took their father."

"You lost them all at once?"

"Within a few days of one another."

"Oh, Edna. I'm so sorry."

"It's long past." Edna stood. "I expect your chowder's cold by now. Let me warm it for you."

Alex frowned. Edna had held so much hurt inside her. Could Alex learn to be that strong as well? To still do good in spite of her pain? Alex sat taller in her chair. "I don't feel up to eating right now. I'll find something later if I get hungry."

"Has that man upset you that much?"

That man? Alex swallowed. Edna's bitterness was natural for someone who loved Alex as much as she did. After all, Alex had had an entire year to come to terms with her feelings and to learn to control her responses. Edna would do the same in time.

Edna patted Alex's shoulder. "Try not to fret, my girl. Things have a way of working out."

"I hope so."

The woman pursed her lips, clicked her tongue against the roof of her mouth, and gave Alex an appraising glance. "I dare say you've not only stopped eating more than is good for you but you haven't been sleeping much either. Your eyes are redder than I've seen them since you first came to live in Watson Manor as a young girl. Tell you what—as I said, Louis has been having nightmares the way he used to in his old home, and I promised him I'd teach him how to lock himself in the nursery. He didn't want me to sleep on his floor the way you and Fay did."

The sound of Louis's sobs in the Godfrey's cellar cringed through Alex. "That's understandable. Locking the door, I mean."

"Yes. But what I'm getting at is why don't you go up to your room and relax for a while? After I've helped Louis, I'll bring you a tray of food. Perhaps you'll be hungry by then. And after you've finished eating, you can crawl into bed—make an early night of it."

Alex smiled a little. It had been a long while since she'd felt so mothered. Perhaps it wouldn't hurt for her to relish it for an evening. "I suppose my problems will still be here in the morning." Would Rick?

"Or maybe they won't seem so bad."

"Like lightning storms?"

"Yes."

Alex stood and hugged Edna. "Thank you," she whispered in her ear.

"You're welcome, my girl."

Chapter 12

ALEX WOKE TO THE familiar lemony scent of the household laundry soap. She was in her old room, lying on her stomach in her old bed. When she'd closed her eyes, her stomach had felt comfortably full of warm clam chowder and freshly made tea, and one of the patchwork quilts her mother had made for her before she'd died had been tucked around her shoulders. That much Alex knew. What she didn't know was why she couldn't open her eyes. Was she still asleep?

Something pressed down on top of her, straddling her feet. *Edna? Is that you?* Alex's lips wouldn't open. She gasped through her nose.

The weight moved—stepped—up to her calves. *Ivy!* Of course. It had to be Ivy.

Alex told her arms to move, but they didn't respond. Her legs felt frozen in place. Was she paralyzed? What was happening?

The weight stepped up to her knees.

That's not Ivy. Its leg span was too wide for a cat. *Who's there? Get off me!*

The weight moved to her thighs . . . to her hips.

Help!

The pressure stayed astride Alex's hips, but something else pushed against the center of her back near her lungs. Goose bumps flashed across her body. Was it a human intruder or—*the Night Hag?*

Anger—or was it terror?—surged through Alex's veins. It couldn't be the Night Hag. Demons, if they were real, didn't have physical bodies. A mouse with a scorpion tail, a glowing cat, luminal mushrooms—these all had tangible forms. Demons did not.

Ivy, jump on it! Alistair, break out of your bottle! Attack whatever is on me! Scratch! Bite!

The weight grew heavier. Alex tried and failed to breathe.

Demons are not made of flesh and bones. They can't kill. Humans are stronger than demons. Leave!

Alex's senses tensed. How could she make that force listen to her?

She focused her thoughts, her breath, every ounce of her energy onto her lips. *Open!* They didn't, but her fingers trembled with the exertion.

Finally, she wiggled her toes. Hope surged through her. She was regaining control of her body. *Get off!*

The pressure steadily lifted from her back.

Go away!

The weight stepped back to her thighs . . . to her knees . . . to her feet. It receded off her.

Alex held her breath. Where was the demon?

Footsteps creaked one after the other across the floorboards away from the bed and to the door.

Lift your head. See who's there.

Alex couldn't move.

The floorboards creaked again.

Alex waited.

Nothing more sounded. Not even the turn of the doorknob or the squeaking of its hinges. Either her threat, if it had been a physical being, was still in the room, or the presence was not a physical entity.

Alex squeezed her eyes closed, clenched the bedding, and waited like that, listening for any further movement, until her strength returned. Nothing more moved, and at last, she opened her eyes. She sat up and placed her feet on the floor. She looked at Ivy, still curled atop the blanket on the chair, at the bureau, at her night robe that she'd draped over the foot of her bed, and at the closed door. All was just as she'd last seen them. Had she only had a nightmare? Or—or perhaps she hadn't been fully awake as she'd thought she was, and her mind had played tricks on her. That had to be it. All the day's talk of murder and the Night Hag must have crept into her dreams. Rick might even be proud of her when he found out she wasn't as lacking in imagination as she'd always claimed to be. *Rick. Was. Leaving.*

Her teeth chattered. She hugged her bed quilt around her body.

But if what had just happened had been a dream, why had she heard, felt, sensed everything around her as if she were awake? More important, why hadn't she been able to move?

She had no answers, but the one thing she did know was sleep would not return until she'd somehow settled her nerves.

Ivy snored.

Alex ran her hands over her face. How could that cat have slept so peacefully while Alex had experienced such terror? On the other hand, if Ivy had wakened to find someone or something out of the ordinary in her room, what would she have done? Would she have raced away in fear? Would she have glowed the way she'd done when they'd heard Louis and Mr. Godfrey's voices from the past?

Alex jumped to her feet. She was being ridiculous. The being—intruder—demon—was most likely nothing more than her overactive imagination. What she needed was a cup of hot, strong, unsweetened tea. The kind Rick had taught her was a remedy for sleeplessness. Tea would be tonight's savior.

She yanked on her night robe, shoved her feet into her slippers, and strode to the door. She grabbed the knob. Stopped.

Yet, was going that moment to the kitchen for tea the wisest course? Yeah, whatever she'd just encountered had most likely been her imagination, but what if it wasn't? What if someone or something was still in the house, waiting in the dark and watching for her?

I can't leave this room.

She huffed.

But I can't just sit here, either. I should . . . what?

Find someone who could ease her troubled mind.

Her first thought went to Uncle Henry, but she immediately discounted him. He would want to help her, but what could he do, weak and unwell as he was? And Edna, her dear comforter, was in the basement with the rest of the staff. Alex would have to make her way through the entire dark house to get to her. That left Rick.

She folded her arms and again paced about the room.

Rick's room was just across the hall. And Uncle Henry did want the two of them to work together. What was more, Rick had experience with otherworldly creatures, which meant he would know exactly what she should do. And his comfort . . . no matter what else happened between them, she could not deny his ability to comfort her was very real.

Alex sighed. She would consult with Rick.

Once again, Alex studied Ivy, who still slept, and went to the door. She inched it open and peeked into the hall. No movement. No sound.

Staring into the blackness, she dashed across the hallway to Rick's bedroom. She tapped on the door. "Rick?" she whispered.

No answer.

She tapped again. "Rick? I'm sorry to wake you."

Still, he didn't answer. No light seeped through the opening beneath his door, either. Was he asleep? Did she dare open the door and wake him?

She winced. She certainly couldn't do that. Such a thing wouldn't be appropriate. And yet, why wouldn't it be? He was her husband.

Alex hugged her arms tightly around her, searched back and forth down each end of the hall, and at last opened the door. "Rick?" she whispered into the shadowed room.

He didn't answer, so she stepped inside and said his name again, louder this time. Still, he didn't answer. He wasn't in the room at all. Though, he had been there, for his morning coat hung in his open wardrobe, and his bedcovers lay in a rumpled heap at the foot of his bed. Where had he gone?

For one mad moment, she wondered if he actually had been her intruder, but she quickly cast that thought away. It wasn't Rick. She knew that as well as she knew any other universal truth. Still, where was he?

She scrutinized the room. As she'd noted before, his morning coat was in his wardrobe, which likely meant he hadn't gone out and was still in the house. She ran her hand over his pillow. It was only a little cool, like it hadn't been that long since someone had occupied it. And an empty teapot and cup lay on the table next to his bed.

Alex furrowed her brows. His having a teakettle in his room wasn't odd. Rick liked tea so well that he often drank several cups of it throughout the day. But he rarely drank it at night, unless . . . her mouth turned dry. Unless he was sick.

Alex tugged her nightrobe tighter around her and hurried from the room. She ran her hand along the wall until she reached the end table at the top of the staircase. No lantern. Had someone—something—taken it?

Shivers shot down her back. *Don't be an idiot! There is no such thing as a Night Hag.* Someone must have needed the lantern. Rick!

She clasped the banister and followed it down to the kitchen in the basement. A stream of light flowed out from beneath the bottom of the kitchen door. A pot clanged. It was much too early for Cook to be starting breakfast, which meant—

She turned the doorknob and stepped inside. A single lantern rested in the center of the worktable, and Rick, behind it, leaned forward with his hands pressed flat against the tabletop. His hair hung limply in front of his face. He wore only his trousers and a white shirt, which was open at the neck down to his sternum.

He looked up. "Alex?"

She hurried to him. Even in the lamplight, his face looked pale. "What's happened? Are you all right?"

"I've got a bug, I think. I thought a cup of tea might settle my stomach." A bowl of tea leaves, an infuser, and an empty water kettle sat on the table in front of him. "I hope I didn't wake you when I passed your room on my way down."

Alex studied Rick's gaunt features and his drooping posture. For a moment, she wondered if he might have seen whoever or whatever had been in her room, but she cast that thought away almost as soon as she had it. If Rick had seen anything, he'd have barged into her room to make sure she was all right. Even if he was sick. "You didn't wake me. I-I had a nightmare. Like you, I came down for some tea."

He held her gaze. Sweat glistened along the top of his forehead. "What was your nightmare? Not the Night Hag, I hope?"

"I don't know what it was. But sit. You look like you're going to collapse at any moment." She stepped next to him, wrapped his arm around her shoulders, and helped him into a chair. "I'll make the tea. You rest. You have a big day tomorrow."

"I do?"

"Whether you travel by horse, train, or coach, you're bound to be tired by the end of it. Being sick will only make it worse."

"What are you talking about?"

"Your treasure. Your partners sent for you, as I recall."

Rick slouched back in his chair and set his forearm on the table. "That. I sent a telegram informing them I'm not ready to go just yet." He looked up at her and held her gaze again. "I told them I have a situation here that still needs—adjusting."

"Oh?" She took the kettle from the table and held it under the water spigot above the sink. "You're not talking about Aunt Pauline's death? Uncle Henry's persistent, but he's also thorough. I really doubt there's anything left for me to find, much less anything to take up more of your time."

Alex set the kettle on the stove, stoked the fire, and headed back to the worktable.

"Alex?" Rick's voice was almost a whisper.

She looked to him. His eyes shone up at her despite the low light. She cleared her throat. "Why don't I tell you about my nightmare while we wait for the tea?"

"Very well. What was it?"

She sat across from him. With Rick in the room, her recounting of the events sounded to her like a made up tale, but when she got to the part about hearing the footsteps creak across the floorboards toward the door, Rick sat taller.

"A week ago, I'd have sworn what you'd experienced was a dream," he said, "but after what we underwent today at the Godfrey home, I'm not sure of anything right now. Do you believe it was a nightmare?"

"I don't know. It seemed so real, and yet when I was finally able to sit up and look around, I found my night robe still lying where I'd put it before retiring. Whatever it was that had climbed on and off my bed would have had to disturb my robe if it had been human, but it didn't look like my robe had been moved at all. You didn't see or hear anyone in the hall when you left your room?"

"No. What about Ivy? Could it have been her? Was she glowing or anything?"

"She was sleeping. No glowing."

Rick placed his hand over Alex's where it rested on the table. "The details have a lot in common with the Night Hag death."

"The Night Hag's not real, if that's what you're thinking."

"Perhaps not, but—" He drew his brows together. "Pauline didn't die of natural causes, as far as the medical examiner could determine, and yet no one found signs of an intruder in her room, either."

The kettle whistled. Alex moved to stand, but Rick's grip tightened around her hand. His gaze deepened.

Sudden heat rose to her cheeks. "What is it?"

"You're so beautiful."

She caught her breath, blinked, and forced a laugh. "This is no time for teasing. I'm in my nightgown, and my hair's a mess."

"You're never a mess."

Alex's muscles stiffened, but she forced another laugh. Compliments often helped Rick work his charm on other people, but they had never worked on her. Had he forgotten that was one of the reasons he liked—used to like—her? "That's not what you were going to say. You're up to something, aren't you?"

"You're right." The edges of his lips tipped upward. "That wasn't what I was going to say. Not then, anyway."

She glanced toward the stove. Why did he keep looking at her like that? Did he have a fever? "I should get the tea. I think you might be sicker than you think."

He released her hand. "Yes. Go."

She stood, took a white teapot from the shelves on the wall at their left, and set the teapot on the work table.

"You're also right about me being up to something." Rick's laugh sounded strained.

"I knew it." She grabbed a hot pad and went to the stove for the water kettle. "All right, what is it?"

"You needn't worry. It's only what I said before. I don't want to give up on us, Alex. I want to come home. To you."

Alex's heartbeat leapt into her throat. She stared at the kettle, but she couldn't think, couldn't make her lips move. "What if that's not what I want?"

"I hoped—what do you want?"

She returned to the worktable. Hot tears burned at the back of her eyes, but she stared hard until they dried there. What she wanted was for Uncle Henry not to die, for Mary not to have died, and for Rick not to have abandoned her, but none of those things were true.

Rick pushed himself to his feet and, after leaning against the chair back another moment, walked toward her until he stood less than a foot away from her. "I love you, Alex. I didn't know it until I climbed into the carriage the day I left, but that's the truth of it."

Alex scooped two spoons full of tea leaves into the infuser and set it in the kettle. She poured steaming water into it and closed the lid. Rick had never lied to her before. His expressions were much too open for him to be good at lying. But even with all those things still true, how could this statement be anything but a lie? "You left," she said.

"I wish I hadn't. I wish—" His gaze wavered. "You needn't worry, Alex. I won't bother you with this, and I won't push, but I believe you should know I'm not willing to give up on us. I have every intention of wooing you the way I should have done in the first place. I want you to be my wife."

Alex's breath stopped. Never had a man said anything even remotely that blunt to her before. Rick hadn't even proposed. His parents and her uncle had simply asked them if they would consider marrying, and they'd agreed. What should she say? How should she feel? "I am your wife."

"Not in your heart. I've missed you, Alex. Everything about you. The way your voice cracks when you wake up in the morning. The—" He swallowed.

She bit the inside of her lower lip. She hated hurting him, and, truth be told, she loved and missed things about him too. She'd even come to realize she couldn't blame him for Mary's death. The past day they'd spent together had taught her he had loved their daughter as much as any father ever loved a daughter. *But* when things got hard, he'd left Alex, and he hadn't come back until her uncle forced the issue. How could she trust him the way a wife needed to trust her husband after such a betrayal? Certainly, sending Vera to her had been a kind gesture, but when looked at in a more prudent light, it had still been a way for him to ease his conscience from a distance. Fay had been right when she'd warned Alex that men like Rick, adventurers, would never be the settling-down kind.

"Friendship is all I want," she said.

"Well, then." Rick inhaled, placed both his hands on her upper arms, and turned her toward him. He kissed her softly on the forehead. "Friends it is—for now."

Her insides rolled over with the physical need she'd only recently realized she had for him, but she kept her expression devoid of feeling. Passivity was her shield. "The tea's ready."

Rick smiled, but his eyes drooped. "We best drink it then. And afterward . . ."

"Afterward?"

"I won't be sleeping for a while, and I doubt you will either. Why don't we take another look at Pauline's room? And bring that cat."

Alex tilted her head. Had he, like her, noticed the connection between Ivy's glowing ability and Louis's sobs in the Godfrey's cellar? "I thought you didn't like her."

"Feelings have a way of changing over time," he said. "I hope."

Chapter 13

Ivy jumped into Alex's arms the moment Alex opened her bedroom door. She shifted the cat to her left arm and took her silk handbag out of the bureau with her right.

Alex handed her handbag to Rick. "The key's in the bottom, but be careful not to stick your finger on my embroidery needle." After all that had happened at the Godfrey's that day, Alex had forgotten to give Edna back the key to Pauline's room.

"Since when did you take up stitching?" Rick set the lantern he'd brought from the kitchen onto the bureau, separated the handbag's drawstrings, and peered inside. He removed a small container and held it up to the light. "Crickets?"

"They're for Alistair." Alex pointed to the jar on top of her wardrobe. "He's sort of Vera's good luck charm. She made me take him with me."

Rick, arching an eyebrow, set the jar of crickets next to Alex's food tray. "And the stitching?"

"Vera only showed me the basics. She thought it might help me keep my mind busy while I was on the train."

"Did it work?"

"Quite well, in fact. The train ride was long enough that I almost finished an entire pillow cover." Alex glanced away from him. "Thank you for Vera, by the way."

"You're welcome." He tilted his head, watching her as he again fumbled through her handbag. "Ouch!"

"I told you to watch out for the needle."

He pulled out his unhurt hand and cradled it, the palm upward, with his other hand. His frown was almost a smile. "I suppose this is the key?"

"You know it is. Please be serious, Rick. This is not a joking matter."

"I am serious. And anyway, serious doesn't mean dead. Sorry. Poor choice of words."

Alex rolled her eyes and followed Rick, who was once more carrying the lantern, into the hall. She closed the door, but when she turned back, Rick's expression pinched. He wrapped his arms around his middle and doubled over.

"Would you please stop chaffing?"

"I'm not chaffing," he said between is teeth. "I thought the tea had fixed whatever had upset my stomach earlier. I guess I was wrong."

Alex placed her hands on her hips and studied his face. His skin had paled and his eyes were dull. "Maybe you should go to bed. This can wait until morning."

"No. It's all right. It'll pass in a minute."

"I'm not so sure you are all right."

Rick pressed his lips into a straight line, eyed Alex out of the corner of his eye, and slowly straightened his spine. His pinched expression softened, but only slightly. Had the sickness actually subsided, or was he only pretending it had?

The two reached Aunt Pauline's bedchamber. Rick unlocked the door, and they stepped inside. This room, the one Aunt Pauline had died in, had originally been a guest room. However, after her quarrel with Uncle Henry, she'd angrily retired there for the night. As such, the room only contained a few of her personal belongings.

Ivy hissed and leapt from Alex's arms to the floor.

"That's odd," Alex said. "Ivy usually won't let go of me, especially in the dark."

"I can't say I blame her for that." Rick set the key on the small table next to the door and walked to the middle of the room. He held the lantern at arm's length in front of him. His hand shook slightly. "Where do you want to start looking?"

The room looked much like her own bedchamber, complete with an unmade bed and a rocking chair. "How can one know if an intruder's been in the room if everything is just as it was when you last saw it?"

"You're thinking of your nightmare."

"Or whatever it was."

Rick sauntered back to Alex. Standing in front of her, he squeezed her upper arms then straightened her night robe's collar. As he did so, his thumb brushed the side of her neck.

Shivers shot through her body. She folded her arms and narrowed her eyes, pretending nothing had unsettled her.

Whether or not she succeeded, she didn't know, for he simply held her gaze. "My only suggestion is we look for something unusual. When my partners and I finally found the burial place for Bavo the Great's lost treasure, we found the blade of a seventeenth-century knife among the surrounding rocks. It's what led us to the treasure."

"What's so unusual about a knife?"

"Not *a* knife. *That* knife. Bavo the Great hid his treasure in the fifteenth century."

"You mean someone got to the treasure before you did."

"That's our deduction."

"But you collected it, didn't you?"

"We did."

"If someone had already been to that tomb, why didn't he take the treasure?"

"We don't know that answer." Rick grinned. "Maybe a demon fed him Monk's Bane, and it killed him before he could get away."

Alex frowned and moved to the window, but when she reached it and Rick could no longer see her face, she smiled. Their bantering was one of the things she had missed. "That's not likely," she said aloud. "And anyway, you know very well that inanimate entities can't kill."

He pursed his lips. "Well then, maybe someone, an actual human, was still guarding the treasure after all that time and killed the earlier robber. I've heard stories of such things."

"A two-hundred-year-old guard?"

"You never know. Maybe he drank an elixir of life." He chuckled.

Alex rolled her eyes and walked to the wardrobe. She opened it.

Someone groaned.

Alex whirled. Rick still stood in the center of the rug.

"Is your stomach bothering you again?" she asked.

"That wasn't me."

"Would you please stop with the jests?"

"This isn't a jest."

The voice groaned again. It was a woman's voice, and it came from the direction of the bed.

Goose bumps flashed over Alex's body. "Ivy!" The cat, her back arched, stood on top of it. Her fur glowed like white light. "Was that you?"

Ivy jumped off the bed and scampered beneath it.

"She's doing it again," Alex said.

"Doing what?"

"Glowing." Alex tapped her forefinger against her pursed lips. "You know, this is the third time that's happened when a voice suddenly came out of nowhere. I'm starting to think Ivy's glowing power has something to do with those voices."

Again, the voice groaned.

Alex's hands turned clammy. She shoved them beneath her folded arms and hunched her shoulders as if she were cold.

Rick clasped her forearm. "Should we leave? We can come back tomorrow—when it's daylight."

Warmth from his touch spread through her, but she shook it off. "Of course not! We've got to investigate that noise *now*."

"That's my girl." He stepped toward the foot of the bed and looked underneath. "Ivy? Where'd you go?" Suddenly, Rick's knees buckled. Gripping the bedpost, he pulled himself onto the mattress, collapsing face-first.

"Rick!" Alex grabbed his shoulders and pulled him around onto his back. She pressed her hand against his forehead, checking for a fever. His skin felt cold. "We've got to get you back to your room and call for a physician." She sat beside him.

A noise sounded outside the door. Was someone out there?

"I'm fine," Rick said. "Whatever it is will pass in a minute."

White light burst from beneath the small table by the door. *So that's where Ivy went.*

A strange, ethereal sound trickled through the air—like metal tinkling against glass—abruptly followed by a loud clatter.

"Dash it all!" a woman's voice said.

Ivy shot across the floor. She leapt into Alex's lap.

More whispery sounds filled the room.

"You coddle the children too much," Aunt Pauline's voice said.

"I'll do better, ma'am," the other woman said.

"See that you do, or I'll have to let you go." Another clinking sound. "There's something wrong with this tea."

"I made it the same as always."

The pouring of liquid and another clink. "Then make it again. No-no! Leave the plant and get me a new cup!"

Ivy circled atop Alex's lap then jumped onto the end table and over to the windowsill. She pressed her body against the glass. The glow disappeared.

Rick took Alex's hand. "Did you recognize those voices?"

"It was only Aunt Pauline and Edna." Alex placed her hand against Rick's cheek. "How are you feeling now?"

He didn't answer, but his gaze intensified.

"Why are you looking at me like that?"

"Did you hear what the voices said?"

For a moment, Alex thought Ivy might leap back onto her lap, but when Ivy instead scampered to the corner chair, Alex steepled her fingers and thought back on what she'd just heard. Groans, dishes, Aunt Pauline and Edna, and . . . Alex caught her breath . . . and Aunt Pauline threatening to let Edna go.

Alex stiffened. "It was only a one time, off-the-cuff threat."

"Are you certain?"

Alex's thoughts flashed over memories from her past. Aunt Pauline had been angry with Alex during much of her first years at Watson

Manor, but Edna had always smoothed things between them. Later, Alex had figured her view of Aunt Pauline had come through child-colored eyes, but now . . . Had Aunt Pauline threatened Edna more than once? Did Edna have—*motive*?

"Don't be ridiculous," Alex said. "We don't even know if what we're hearing are true events. Maybe it's a trick of some kind." She rubbed the back of her neck. The office, the cellar, this room. Could a cat be a ventriloquist?

"You know as well as I do it wasn't a trick. Ivy is not a witch. We know what we heard in the office came from a real event. And the words and emotions we heard in the Godfrey's cellar felt too strong, too painful, and so fully authentic that we couldn't possibly deny their reality. That tells me . . ."

"That this is also real," Alex cut it.

"I know it's hard, luv, but we have to accept it. The dinner dishes, the voices, even the dead plant your uncle listed in his file—all of them make sense when connected with Edna."

Alex shook her head. This couldn't be true. *Please, God, don't let it be true.* "What do the dead plants have to do with anything?" she snapped, grasping at threads, hoping they were ropes.

"It sounded as if your aunt poured the tea on the plant. The tea Edna gave her."

Alex blinked. Her thoughts flashed from images of simple, refreshing tea to the deadly scent of "Monk's Bane. Monk's Bane tea can kill plants."

Rick nodded.

"But a dead plant isn't physical proof of—of anything."

"Maybe not." Rick smiled sadly. "But I think you'll soon have more than enough proof."

"What do you mean?"

"Edna brought me a dinner tray this evening."

"What of it? She brought me one too."

"I can't move my legs, Alex."

"What?" Alex grabbed Rick's calves. Even through his pants, his legs felt more like stiff clay than warm flesh. "I'll send a servant for the doctor."

"Stay here," Rick said. "The cold is quickly crawling up my body. I'm afraid I won't be here when you return, and I'd rather you were here when—"

Alex froze.

"—I'd rather not die alone." He collapsed onto the bed.

"Rick!" Alex grabbed his arm and rolled him onto his back. "Stop this, you hear me? You're not going to die!"

The door opened, and Edna walked into the room. She softly closed the door behind her, locked it with the key Rick had left on the end table, and slid that key into her front apron pocket. She took a deep, satisfied breath. "Yes, he will, my girl."

Chapter 14

"THERE'S NO NEED FOR you to worry," Edna continued. "Mr. Dalton will die, and you will find happiness again."

"What are you talking about? I don't want Rick to die. And I certainly won't be happy if he does." Alex rushed to Edna and grabbed both her shoulders. Rick's talk about poison was nonsense. This was Edna—her Edna—the woman who'd cared for her after her own mother had died. "We have to stop whatever's happening to him. Please help me, Edna."

Edna's blue eyes sparked in the lamplight. "I'm sorry, my girl. We can't stop the poison. But you needn't worry. This is the right course. He won't be able to hurt you anymore."

Ivy jumped onto the bed next to where Rick lay. Her fur lit up like a ball of lightning.

"What is this?" Aunt Pauline's voice whispered over the air.

"Something to help you sleep," Edna's long-ago voice said.

"I don't want to sleep!"

Glass crashed.

"Pouring the rest out won't stop the Monk's Bane," Edna's voice said. "You already feel it, don't you?"

Cold plummeted through Alex's core. She clenched Edna's arms. "You killed Aunt Pauline?"

"Yes, dear."

"How could you?"

Edna smiled gently. "I loved you. Loved Fay. I couldn't let her keep hurting the two of you."

Rick groaned. It was a rough, guttural sound that rumbled from deep inside him, pulling, it seemed, at a similar place inside Alex. She hurried back to him and placed her hand on top of where his hand rested on his stomach. His fingers felt like dry icicles.

"Please, Edna," Alex said. "Tell me how to help him!"

Edna clasped Alex's shoulder. "It's best to just let it be, my girl. See how it is with Louis? He struggles some, but he is better off without that man, and he knows it. You will soon know the same peace too."

"What are you saying?"

"She's saying she killed Mr. Godfrey as well as your aunt," Rick whispered. He struggled to sit upright but finally flopped back against the bed.

Alex clasped Rick's cold hand in both of hers and gaped up at her beloved nanny. Edna, not Louis, must have been responsible for the dead plant she and Rick had found at the Godfrey's house. And the ants. "You couldn't have killed that man," she said, hoping it was true yet fearing it wasn't. "You didn't even know Jeremiah Godfrey."

"I'd seen enough of him at community events and such, how he treated Louis, and how the boy feared him. He was just like Pauline. Like my mother too. They all had the same evil in their eyes. You understand me, don't you, my girl? I couldn't bear to see that evil any longer. Their eyes had to close forever, and I knew how to make that happen."

Alex's fingers trembled. She couldn't blink, could hardly breathe, but at the same time hot and protective anger built up inside her like a keg of pressurized explosives. Something was wrong with Edna. Maybe she needed a doctor's care. But Alex could not—would not—let whatever that wrongness was kill Rick. She scanned the room. She had to find a way to get them out of there before he—*No! Rick will not die!*

Rick must have read her expression, because he slipped his hand out from under hers and placed it on top of her forearm. His touch was cooler than usual, but it was still steady and calm. He was dying, yet he was still trying to comfort her.

"Did you mix the poison in their food like you did mine?" Rick asked Edna.

"It was easy enough to slip the Monk's Bane into Mr. Godfrey's refreshment after the ball game," Edna said. "It doesn't mix as well in lemonade as it does in tea, but as you shall soon see, both liquids can do the job."

Alex stood, whirled, and stood like a shield in front of Rick. "Edna! Richard Dalton is my husband."

Edna slowly shook her head. "Your marriage is only a temporary inconvenience, my girl. I learned two things when my mother cultivated Monk's Bane and poisoned my brothers and sister with it. I think, as a scientist, you will understand such learning."

Alex's insides cringed backward, but she stiffened her stance. She glanced at the locked door. "Tell me how to save him."

"The first thing I learned," Edna said, "is if I could overcome my fear enough to take daily sips of Monk's Bane tea, I could develop an immunity to it. I sometimes wonder if my mother died proud of what I'd learned or angry because I had rid myself of her before she'd rid herself of me." Edna sighed. "And two, one needn't be bound to misery all of one's life. A person can make changes. I'm helping you make those changes."

Alex lunged toward the door, but Edna stopped her mid stride. Her grip viced around her arm. Had the woman always been that strong?

"Did you poison my food too?"

"Just enough to calm you so you could sleep through the night."

"Sleep? I had a nightmare!"

"Oh, dear. Of the night hag? Forgive me, my girl. That can happen sometimes. My dose must have been too strong. Well, you're over it now, so no harm done."

The hair on the back of Alex's neck stood. "I won't let you kill Rick." She yanked her arm from Edna's grasp and raced to the door. She pounded on it, turned the knob back and forth. "Help! We need a doctor! Someone get the police."

Edna squeezed Alex's shoulder and pulled her away from the door. "There's no need to make such a fuss, my girl. Mr. Dalton will be gone in a few minutes, and everything will be put right. Why don't you let me make you some tea to calm your nerves until he is gone?" She chuckled. "I don't mean Monk's Bane tea, of course."

"I don't want more tea." Alex rushed back to Rick and again placed the back of her hand against his forehead. Though sweat pooled along his hairline, his skin felt even cooler than before. She pulled a folded blanket out from under his feet and draped it over him.

"Thank you, luv." His whisper faded into a groan.

"Please let me out of here, Edna. I've got to get *help*." She yelled that last word. "Can't you see how wrong this is?"

Edna took the chair above where Ivy hid—Ivy scrambled under the bureau—and slid it next to the door. She sat and clasped her hands in her lap. "Destroying those who hurt us isn't wrong, my girl. It's a blessing."

Rick coughed. Alex slid her arm under his shoulders, lifted him slightly upright, and pulled the blanket to his mouth. Perhaps the warm air would soothe his cough.

"I love you." Rick's mouth barely moved, but his eyes clung to Alex's gaze. She touched the artery at his throat and pressed her hand against his chest. His heart still pulsed, but not strongly the way she remembered it. She had to do something to help him *now* or it would soon be too late, but what?

Her mind raced over every plant she knew, both natural and luminal. Crimsonica? It could pull heat out of the earth, but could it pull poison from a body? Syllitac? What about Aloe vera? Nothing. *No, there has to be something!* Her thoughts paused. *In my room!*

Alex laid Rick against the pillow and charged at Edna. She grabbed her arms. "You know that poison. You must know its antidote."

Edna broke free from Alex's grasp and slapped her across the face. "There is no antidote! Now sit down and calm yourself. I taught you to behave better than that."

Alex fell backward. Her head hit the table next to the bed. Her ears rang.

"Oh, my dearest girl!" Edna got up from the chair and bent over her. She clasped her hand between hers. "You startled me, and—please forgive me."

Alex gaped. Were those real tears in Edna's eyes? After all Edna had done, did she truly care for her? If so, maybe Alex could manipulate that affection. "Edna, please don't let Rick die. He and I have had troubles, it's true, but he's my friend—the best friend I've ever had. If you kill him, *you* will hurt me more than anyone ever has."

Edna's pupils wavered. Her cheeks blanched. "Don't lie to me."

Alex pushed herself to her feet. "I'm not lying."

Edna edged backward. She shook her head. "It's not true. You hate him. You want to be rid of him."

No longer thinking, only feeling, Alex gathered all her pent-up emotions, sat next to Rick, and kissed him squarely on the mouth. Rick's hands moved to her waist, but she didn't flinch. Instead, she slid her arms tightly around his neck and pressed her body against his. His hands moved weakly to her back. Their lips clung together. They clung so long that loneliness Alex hadn't known she felt surged from within her. Tears filled her eyes.

At last, she pulled away from him. His gaze bore into hers but she looked at Edna. Edna's chin quivered.

"Please, Edna. I love him."

"Alex," Rick whispered. "I. Can hardly. Breathe."

Alex grabbed Edna's arm. "Help him, please. Don't do this."

Edna shook her head. "It's too late."

Something crashed outside the door, followed by thuds.

"Help!" Alex ran for the door. "Please, help!" But before she reached it, Edna stepped in front of her.

Someone rattled the doorknob. "Mrs. Dalton!" a young voice shouted. "Are you in there?"

Louis.

"Go back to bed, my boy," Edna said with only a hint of inflection. "The cat's causing a bit of a ruckus, but everything's alright. We're sorry we woke you."

"Don't listen to her," Alex screamed. "Get help."

Again, Louis twisted the knob, but it clinked and turned uselessly.

"Go!" Alex repeated.

"Yes, son. Go back to bed. I'll bring you some tea in a few minutes."

"You wouldn't!" Alex said.

Louis's footsteps ran down the hall.

Edna rolled her eyes. "Not Monk's Bane, my girl. Just something to help him sleep."

The way she'd helped me to sleep. Alex scowled. At the same time, her mind raced. How could she get past Edna and unlock the door?

Ivy.

The cat could be both a weapon and a shield. Her luminal abilities might even provide a crucial distraction.

Alex lunged toward Edna. Ivy, next to her feet, arched her back and hissed at Edna. In one swift motion, Alex scooped up the cat and hurled her. Ivy let out a sharp yowl. She extended her claws, twisted mid-air, and landed feet-first on Edna's shoulders.

Edna cried out. She raised her arms, protecting her face from Ivy's claws, and Alex lunged forward. She shoved Edna hard. Edna stumbled backward, lost her balance, and toppled over the rocking chair. Then, before Edna could recover, Alex searched Edna's apron pocket and retrieved the cold metal key.

Without hesitation, Alex pushed the chair on top of Edna, buying herself precious seconds, and ran to the door. Fighting to steady her trembling fingers, she jammed the key into the lock. The mechanism resisted. It scraped against the metal. "Come on, come on," Alex muttered.

Edna grunted. "Get this thing off of me!"

Again, Alex twisted the key. This time, the lock clicked. She turned the knob and opened the door.

Louis stood there. He held a heavy candlestick over his head, as if it were a weapon.

Alex rushed into the hall past him. Out of the corner of her eye, she saw Uncle Henry's frail form struggling toward them. "Go back to your rooms and lock yourselves in," she said to both of them, but neither obeyed, and Alex didn't have time to make them do so.

She ran to her bedchamber. Behind her, Louis cried out, and something heavy fell, followed by a brief, muffled struggle.

Alex, inside her room, grabbed Alistair's jar from the top of the wardrobe and returned to Aunt Pauline's room. There, Edna lay slumped against the wall, tightly bound with window sashes, and a corner of a blanket stuffed in her mouth. Uncle Henry, looking pale but determined, leaned against the wall next to the bed where Rick lay unconscious. And Louis, still holding his makeshift weapon, stood guard over the lot of them.

"Is Mr. Dalton dying?" Louis asked.

"No." Alex opened the specimen jar and dumped the tarantula onto Rick's leg. "Alistair will make certain of that." *Please, God.*

Chapter 15

SHORTLY BEFORE SUNRISE THE next morning, Rick convinced Alex to put Alistair back in his jar. He was well now, as she could certainly see, and he didn't need a big, hairy spider to bite him yet a third time.

"I'm not sure the doctor will agree with you," Alex jested.

After the police had arrived and taken Edna into custody, and after the physician had declared that all Rick needed was a good night's rest, Uncle Henry and Louis had returned to their rooms.

Alex sat on the bed next to Rick, and Ivy, snoring softly, lay curled in her lap. "When I said good-bye to the doctor at the door a few minutes ago, he seemed quite impressed with Alistair. He asked if he could have one of his offspring—if Vera ever finds him an appropriate mate."

"How romantic." Rick shifted his shoulders against the pillow. "Would you mind helping me sit up?"

"Just a minute." Alex set Ivy on the cushion and returned to Rick's side. She, leaning over him, slid her right arm beneath his shoulders, lifted him, and plumped his pillow. "How's that?"

His eyes, his face, his lips were so close to hers that all she could think about was their kiss. The one she'd deceived Edna with. The one that hadn't meant anything. Had it? She stood.

"So you love me?" he said.

Alex bit her lip. "I had to do—say—something to convince Edna to save you, didn't I?"

"You convinced me."

Alex studied him. In the hours after the police had taken Edna away, and after Alistair had saved Rick's life, she had thought on everything Rick had said and done since their meeting with Uncle Henry. A small part of her hoped he truly wanted to return to her, but a larger, more cautious part feared he would ultimately leave again.

"I'll admit you're my best friend," she said, "but I also recognize you might not have been thinking clearly when we talked in the kitchen. What I'm saying is, I know how important your work is to you, Rick, and I will not hold you to—to the idea that we could start again, or even that we could be friends the way we used to be."

Rick shifted taller against his pillow. "I meant what I said, Alex. Yes, my work is important to me, but so are you. And so is Mary. I'm determined you and I will work this out."

She swallowed. Five years of marriage—six if she counted the year he'd been away—had taught her people did not change easily. "It might be too late for us."

"I don't believe it." He motioned to the jar with Alistair inside. "At any rate, if there's anything that tarantula has taught me, it's that some things are worth any risk. *You* are worth any risk."

The two stared at one another, and the air seemingly pulsed around them.

"You do realize Ivy might be the key," he said, breaking the silence.

"To what?"

"Finding Mary's murderer. Maybe whoever it was left traces when he took her. That's what you're hoping to find with those mushrooms, isn't it? Physical traces? Perhaps Ivy can bring out emotional ones."

Alex widened her eyes. Once again, her thoughts raced over the times when Ivy had glowed, and especially when luminal voices had revealed moments from the past. "Emotional traces? That's genius. Great deduction, Rick. But I don't think Ivy's power will help us. She's already been at the yard where you last saw Mary and down by the river where the police found her body. Ivy didn't glow. And she certainly didn't bring out long-ago voices."

"Maybe there's someplace else we can try. Someplace we don't know about."

"Perhaps." Alex turned away from him and headed for the door. She'd reflect on that idea later, but for now she needed to collect Joe Pye weeds. Warmth and movement had returned to Rick's legs, but his chill had turned to a fever; he needed Joe Pye tea to cool it.

"You'll be back?" Rick's voice tilted upward in the way he knew both provoked and challenged her.

Alex clenched the doorknob. Friendly wickedness rushed through her. The best way to confront one of Rick's taunts had always been to tease him back with something strong enough to stop his thoughts. "Soon," she said without looking back at him. "But with something else that bites."

He caught his breath, and Alex grinned at the door.

"Please, not another spider," Rick said.

Slowly, Alex faced him. Then, holding his gaze with the same unwavering look he'd given her several times over the last couple of days, she returned to his side and gently kissed him on the forehead. "You'll have to wait and see," she whispered.

His mouth dropped open, and she, smiling, turned and left the room.

The End—for now

COMING SOON!

Dalton and Dalton Mysteries, Book 2

Sneak peek:

Her mystiobiological research uncovered more than she bargained for. Now, with a child's life at stake and a killer on the loose, Alex will discover that the one man she'd sworn to keep at a distance now becomes her only hope of survival.

Did you like *Moonlight and Monk's Bane*?

If so, go here: https://www.amazon.com/review/create-review?asin=B0DWLRBWD9

or scan the QR code to leave a review on Amazon. It only takes a few minutes, authors really appreciate it, and it helps readers find books they might like. Thanks!

About Ronda Gibb Hinrichsen

A WARD-WINNING AUTHOR RONDA GIBB Hinrichsen lives between the beautiful Rocky Mountains and the Great Salt Lake, where she regularly sees eagles, hawks, owls, and ducks. Lots of ducks. She has had dozens of fiction and nonfiction published in magazines, and she is the author of mystery romance and fantasy novels. She also writes children's fantasy under the pen name of R.K. Grant. Ronda loves reading, writing, and music, though not necessarily in that order, and she enjoys traveling with her husband throughout the world in search of fascinating stories and settings. She loves hearing from readers, and you can contact her at ronda@rondahinrichsen.com.

To learn more about Ronda, visit her website at rondagibbhinrichsen.com. You can also connect with her on her Amazon page, Facebook, Bookbub, and Instagram.